How had sh

Then she remembered. Their sleds had collided, and after rolling in the snow she'd landed in a heap right on top of him.

Once he regained his footing, he reached down to clasp her outstretched hand.

"Easy there. It's slick here."

She'd barely stood when her footing gave way and she pitched forward into his chest, her arms flying around him to stay upright. And then she looked up at him, eyes wide, her face mere inches from his.

"I'm…sorry." Why had her words come out a breathy whisper?

Up close, the depths of his stormy gray eyes were even more amazing than she'd remembered. For a long moment they stared at each other.

What was she doing? Garrett was a friend. Just a friend. She stepped back sharply. "I think I have my footing now."

So why was her heart still pounding?

Glynna Kaye treasures memories of growing up in small Midwestern towns—and vacations spent with the Texan side of the family. She traces her love of storytelling to the times a houseful of great-aunts and great-uncles gathered with her grandma to share candid, heartwarming, poignant and often humorous tales of their youth and young adulthood. Glynna now lives in Arizona, where she enjoys gardening, photography and the great outdoors.

Books by Glynna Kaye

Love Inspired

Hearts of Hunter Ridge

Rekindling the Widower's Heart
Claiming the Single Mom's Heart
The Pastor's Christmas Courtship

Dreaming of Home
Second Chance Courtship
At Home in His Heart
High Country Hearts
A Canyon Springs Courtship
Pine Country Cowboy
High Country Holiday

The Pastor's Christmas Courtship

Glynna Kaye

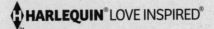
HARLEQUIN® LOVE INSPIRED®

Recycling programs
for this product may
not exist in your area.

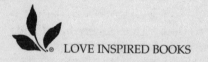

LOVE INSPIRED BOOKS

ISBN-13: 978-0-373-81945-4

The Pastor's Christmas Courtship

www.Harlequin.com

Printed in U.S.A.

And without faith it is impossible to please God, because anyone who comes to him must believe that he exists and that he rewards those who earnestly seek him.
—*Hebrews* 11:6

Let the morning bring me word of your unfailing love, for I have put my trust in you. Show me the way I should go, for to you I entrust my life.
—*Psalms* 143:8

Let us draw near to God with a sincere heart and with the full assurance that faith brings, having our hearts sprinkled to cleanse us from a guilty conscience and having our bodies washed with pure water. Let us hold unswervingly to the hope we profess, for he who promised is faithful.
—*Hebrews* 10:22–23

To Natasha Kern—
my agent, encourager and sister in Christ.

Chapter One

❧

"Could you use some help there, ma'am?"

Ma'am? Her hooded head jerking up, Jodi Thorpe grimaced at the sound of a male voice carrying over the rumble of a big diesel pickup. Headlights illuminating the lingering remnants of twilight, the truck idled alongside her on the snow-covered dirt road. The passenger-side window had been rolled down, but the driver calling out from the far side of the interior was cloaked in shadow, behind a veil of steadily falling snow.

Exactly what she didn't need—a small-town Good Samaritan.

"Thanks for the offer," she responded at a volume she hoped could be heard as she gave the tow rope attached to a four-foot-long, molded plastic toboggan another tug, "but I'm fine, thanks."

She waved the man off with a mittened hand and trudged on, grateful for the snow glow reflecting off the lowered clouds. Without it, it would be impossible to keep her footing on the rutted shoulder of a ponderosa pine–lined road.

Maybe a December getaway to her family's soon-to-be-sold mountain cabin in Hunter Ridge, Arizona, wasn't such a good idea after all. But with her parents out of the country, the opportunity for a quiet retreat seemed ideal. Not only for soul-searching time alone—Decembers were always a bittersweet reminder of the precious life she'd once carried inside her—but to spare her two Phoenix-based sisters from having to host her for the holidays. Why put a damper on their and their children's Christmas festivities?

"Ma'am?"

The man sounded as if he were addressing someone twice her age. But bundled in an oversize insulated coat and clunky boots she'd found in the cabin—and burdened by a backpack—she probably did look like a hunched-over crone of fairy-tale fame.

"I can throw that stuff in the back of my truck," the voice came again as the pickup crept along beside her. "And take you to wherever it is you're headed."

She stiffened. Like she was going to climb into a vehicle with someone she didn't know? The trusting brown eyes of Anton Garcia flashed through her mind. If only years ago she'd overcome her fear of telling him the truth, had accepted his marriage proposal. And if only he hadn't volunteered to hitchhike for help on that deserted Mexican road.

Why, God?

Taking a steadying breath, she yelled over the rumbling engine. "Thanks, but I'm almost there."

She could see the cabin's porch light not too far in the distance as she dragged behind her the bright red toboggan she'd often ridden as a kid. Its load of groceries and other supplies hadn't seemed cumbersome when she'd started back to the cabin, nor the journey ahead of her long. Growing up, she and her younger sisters had often traversed this route to run errands for their grandmother. But now her fingers had stiffened with cold and her arm strained at the bulky weight.

"You're going to hurt yourself, ma'am."

Enough of the "ma'am" business. Wanting to get away from the self-proclaimed Boy Scout—*or was he only pretending to be a holiday helper?*—she gave the tow rope an extra-hearty tug. The toboggan held fast to whatever abruptly anchored it under the frosty mantle and tipped sideways, spilling its load and jerking the rope from her hand. Thrown off balance, she toppled into the snow.

The sound of a truck door slamming tipped her off that the driver had exited his vehicle. Trying not to panic, she struggled to sit upright, but the weight of the backpack rendered her as helpless as a turtle on its back.

"Let me help you up." Through the falling snow, she detected the man reaching out his gloved hand. What choice did she have but to accept his assistance?

Please God, let him be a good guy. After all, it's only two weeks until Christmas. And despite what You may have heard my sisters say, I'm not a Grinch, a Scrooge or anything of the kind.

Not much, anyway.

Reluctantly, she grasped the hand that stretched out to steady her as she staggered ungracefully to her feet. Her hood fell back, snowflakes pelting her face and the cold wind penetrating her long hair.

"Jodi?" The man's voice held an incredulous note. "Jodi Thorpe?"

She blinked, trying to focus through the falling snow.

"Garrett?" In a community of under two thousand residents, why did Garrett McCrae have to be her rescuer tonight? And what was he doing in a town he vowed never to return to once he could make his escape?

"Yeah, it's me, Jodi."

A familiar grin lit his face, and for a horrifying moment she thought he was going to hug her. But something in her eyes as she mentally flew back through time must have halted him. He plunged his hands into the pockets of his navy down jacket and took a step back, his eyes searching her face as intently as hers searched his.

Even though she and Garrett had been the best of friends as kids when she and her two younger sisters visited their grandparents' vacation home in the mountains, she hadn't seen or spoken to him in a dozen years. Not since that last ill-fated night when he'd crushed her teenage dream of them ever being more than friends.

But time had treated him well. Gone was the ponytailed hair that as a teen had nearly splintered his relationship with his dad, replaced by a conservative cut. Lines etched the corners of his eyes, evidence his sense of humor and love of the sunny outdoors had prevailed. His shoulders were impossibly broad. And those eyes… the same deep gray she too-well remembered.

"What are you doing in Hunter Ridge?" they said in unison. Apparently he was as thunderstruck by her presence in town as she was his.

"I'm working here. For a while at least." His brows raised. "And you?"

"I'm helping my folks get my grandparents' cabin ready to sell." At least that was the excuse she intended to use for camping out here until after the holidays. Nobody needed to know the mixed-up mess of the rest of it.

"So, you've been living—where? Married, with a houseful of kids, I suppose."

Her smile threatened to falter, but she held it steady. "None of the above. I'm living in Philadelphia, actually, where I'm a project manager for an athletic apparel company. SmithSmith. And yourself? Still river-running?"

It was a wild guess. Becoming a river guide was all he'd talked about after his first Colorado River rafting trip when he was sixteen, and her grandma had said he'd taken off for training right after high school graduation. So why should she be surprised to find him here in December? Most rafting companies operated with a full crew only in the summer. He probably worked at the family business in the off-season.

"It was the adventure of a lifetime while it lasted." A fleeting shadow flickered through his eyes, then he shrugged. "But I gave it up a while back."

At two years her senior, he would have recently turned thirty, an age that at one time appalled them both as prehistoric. Had a domestically inclined wife lured him away from his youthful obsession? "In other words, old man that you are now, you've turned river-running over to the younger generation?"

"Ouch!" His yelp was accompanied by an exaggerated flinch. Then he laughed that familiar laugh, and her heart inexplicably leaped. Why had she so easily fallen into teasing him just as she'd once done as his tomboy sidekick? They'd long ago left those days behind.

He openly studied her, and despite the chill air, her face warmed. Did he remember that night, too? She motioned briskly to the groceries strewn in the snow. "You're responsible for this. If you hadn't been stalking me, I—"

"Stalking you? I was trying to help you. 'Tis the season. You know, ho ho ho?" Before she could stop him, he snagged the toboggan in one hand and one of her grandma's now partially filled grocery tote bags in another and slung them into the back of his pickup with what looked to be a dwindling load of firewood.

"What are you doing?"

"What's it look like? Getting you and your stuff out of the cold." He squatted to gather the scattered contents back into the other bags. Lifting a cereal box, he waggled it at her. "Still into Cheerios, I see."

With a laugh, she snatched it out of his hand, recalling the afternoon that as an elementary schooler she'd been dared to sneak a family-size cereal box from Grandma's pantry and devour the whole thing herself. Garrett couldn't stop snickering when Grandma insisted she still clean her plate at suppertime.

"You don't need to do this, Garrett. I'm almost there."

"So indulge me." He held out his hand for the cereal box.

What would be the point in arguing? Used to getting his own way, the high-spirited Garrett had long marched to the beat of his own drummer. She'd once foolishly hoped they were marching to the same beat…but learned a hard, humiliating lesson. Except for that out-of-the-blue instance that he made no secret of immediately regretting, he'd never considered her as more than a pal. A buddy.

As soon as he'd stowed the last of her bags, he helped her off with her backpack and opened the passenger-side door. But before she could hoist herself up, a vehicle coming from the opposite direction pinned them in its lights, then pulled parallel to Garrett's truck.

A ball-capped male poked his head out an open pickup window. "I should have figured I'd find you out here rescuing a pretty damsel in distress. Way to go, Preacher."

Jodi turned toward Garrett, catching his deer-in-the-headlights look of alarm.

Preacher?

Uncomfortably conscious of Jodi's questioning gaze, Garrett raised his voice over the rumble of the two vehicles. "Do me a favor, cuz, and keep this to yourself."

"You can count on it." The other man chuckled, then offered a parting wave as he guided his vehicle on down the snowy road.

Garrett didn't meet Jodi's eyes as he held out his hand to assist her into the truck, taking note of the curtain of straight red-blond hair now lightly dusted with snow. It would be too much to hope that she hadn't caught Grady's preacher remark. Nothing much ever got past Jodi, but she'd probably think it was a joke. Some days he wasn't sure if that might be the case. God's little joke, anyway.

As she settled herself in to secure her seat belt, he wedged the backpack at her feet. Then he shut the door and jogged around the front of the vehicle to climb aboard.

"Which cousin was that?"

She'd remembered he had a bunch. "Grady Hunter, the twins' next-to-oldest brother. Luke, Claire and Bekka are all married, and Grady's getting hitched in February. Rio's still single."

She nodded thoughtfully, as if placing long-forgotten faces to the names, maybe recalling that his mother was a sister to the dad of those cousins. He started the truck slowly down the road, its windshield wipers working overtime against the descending snow.

Thankfully, Garrett could trust his cousin to keep his mouth shut. He sure didn't need questions raised about his personal conduct because he'd stopped to assist an old friend. This past year he'd toed a fine line as interim pastor of Christ's Church of Hunter Ridge—as a *single* interim pastor, to be exact.

That was a slippery slope in a place used to family men. He couldn't afford to leave doors open for criticism of his actions if he hoped to qualify for a spot on a highly-thought-of missions team. He was *so* close and needed a positive recommendation from church leadership to seal the deal.

But this was *Jodi*.

He couldn't leave her stranded on a night like this because someone might not think it acceptable for him to escort her home alone. After all, they'd grown up like brother and sister, right?

Nevertheless, his ears warmed as he shoved away a memory he hoped she had no recollection of—although, from the look on her face when she'd recognized him, the odds of that were slim to none. He was pretty sure her grandma, rest her soul, hadn't forgotten. He'd certainly received a well-deserved earful when she'd walked in on them that Christmas Eve. Thankfully, things hadn't gotten beyond hot and heavy kissing. But he probably still owed Jodi a long-overdue apology.

He adjusted the windshield wiper speed. "What are you doing out here in the dark pulling that sled? Where's your car?"

"I use public transportation—and I didn't want to mess with renting a car." Her words came almost reluctantly, as if uncertain how much to share with him. "The forecast showed flurries the next few weeks, so I thought I could get around on one of the bikes at the cabin. I caught a shuttle from the Phoenix airport this afternoon."

Assuming they still lived in the Valley of the Sun, why hadn't she spent the night with her folks or one of her sisters?

"When I got here," she continued, "I made a mistake of stretching out for an intended quick nap. Only I woke up not long before sunset to several inches of snow. Who knows what it will be like tomorrow? So off I went."

He glanced at her, hoping she'd elaborate on what she'd been doing with her life. But she didn't. Incredibly, she wasn't married, but were her sisters? Did her university professor folks still take short-term mission trips during semester breaks? It saddened him that the cabin was to be sold, although to his knowledge the family hadn't gathered there as a whole since her grandma's health abruptly deteriorated and she eventually passed away.

Jodi's mitten-clad hand patted the dashboard. "What's with the monster truck?"

"A loaner from Hunter's Hideaway." That was the family business that had catered to outdoor enthusiasts since early in the last century. "With this cold snap, Grady and I've been delivering firewood to those in need."

She laughed. "So you *are* a do-gooder now."

Did she have to sound so surprised? Admittedly, growing up he'd been forever into mischief. Always pushing boundaries and looking for a good time wherever he could find it. Not a whole lot into thinking of others. But still…

"You even took time from your do-gooder efforts," she noted, "to help this poor old lady stumbling along the side of the road."

"You gotta admit you looked the part." But she sure didn't right now, with that silky hair cascading around her shoulders and a smile lighting her brown eyes. Those very assets had been his downfall the night a transformed sixteen-year-old Jodi showed up in town after a few years' absence, leaving him stupefied and devoid of common sense.

Sort of how he was feeling at this very moment.

Not good.

After his most recent disappointment in the romance department, he'd steered clear of serious involvements. And for an interim pastor, this wasn't a good time to start rethinking that choice. So why had it popped into his head that her arrival in town might be the answer to a prayer he'd uttered but twenty minutes ago?

His office assistant Melody Lenter—an energetic lady about his mom's age—had called around lunchtime, informing him her father in Texas had a heart attack and she and her husband were on their way out of town. She'd have to bail out on overseeing the annual Christmas project she'd single-handedly spearheaded for the past twenty years. Between wood deliveries, he'd spent the afternoon phoning church members, trying to find someone to fill her shoes—but to no avail. He'd barely called out to God that *someone* had to cover for Melody—he sure couldn't take on one more thing—when the capable and ever-dependable Jodi appeared on his doorstep.

Answered prayer? Or a desperate, not-too-bright idea?

"So where's the motorcycle? And—" She

peeked at the back of his head. "What happened to the ponytail?"

Although still waiting for her to zero in on Grady's "preacher" comment, he managed a laugh. "The tail's a thing of the past. I have an SUV now, but a motorcycle's stashed for the winter in a Hunter's Hideaway barn."

The motorcycle made some in his congregation uneasy, which wasn't surprising considering the noisy nuisance he'd made with one as a teenager. No doubt he hadn't been high on the church's interviewee preferences list for a few members. But his Grandma Jo, a force to be reckoned with, convinced them—and him—that his filling in while they searched for a permanent ministerial replacement would benefit all involved.

Coming back, though, hadn't been easy. Nobody in town had a clue what it took to regularly face his old friend Drew Everton and the accusing stares of those who held him responsible for Drew's debilitating injuries. While Drew insisted he wasn't to blame, others weren't so forgiving.

But his year's commitment at Christ's Church would be up at the end of the month, and he was more than ready to move on. Ready to live the dream Drew had been forced to abandon.

"Here we are." He turned the truck into a pine-lined lane leading up to the Thorpe cabin, a wave of nostalgia washing through him as it often did when he drove by. While the porch light lent a cheery note this evening, in broad daylight the place always struck him as melancholy. Lifeless. Although a guy at the church kept an eye on it, that didn't make up for the absence of the warm hospitality and sound of laughter he remembered. Or for missing familiar faces peeping from the dormered attic windows and the sight of his and Jodi's grandmas relaxing on the broad front porch.

He turned to Jodi. "I felt really bad when I heard your grandma passed away." He couldn't imagine not having his Grandma Jo or Grandma McCrae around. That was one of the blessings of Hunter Ridge he'd sorely miss when he left.

"It's funny," Jodi said as she unbuckled her seat belt, "but even though I haven't been here since high school, when I arrived I almost expected to see her step out on the porch to give me a big hug."

"Smelling of freshly baked cupcakes and that honeysuckle hand lotion she always used."

Surprise lit her eyes. "You remember that?"

"I remember a lot of happy times at this cabin."

While his younger sister and Jodi's siblings gravitated to each other to do girlie things, he and Jodi had teamed up to shoot baskets, climb trees and build woodland forts. It was difficult to reconcile memories of the somewhat stout, rough-

and-tumble freckle-faced tomboy of his youth with the sixteen-year-old beauty who'd blindsided his eighteen-year-old self—and with the woman who sat beside him now.

"What do you say we get your stuff inside?"

But *should* he ask her if she could spare time for a project her grandma had at one time helped with—providing Christmas cheer for unwed mothers in the region?

Still undecided, he watched as she retrieved the backpack at her feet. Then just as he gave up on the idea and reached for the door handle, her gentle hand settled on his forearm, her eyes sparkling with mischief.

"Thank you—*Preacher.*"

Chapter Two

It was all Jodi could do to get those words out with a straight face. Garrett would be the last man on earth to be mistaken for minister material. But there it was again—that same caught-in-the-act look she'd seen earlier. What on earth had Garrett been up to that his cousin would mockingly call him "preacher"?

He released his grasp on the door handle, his expression uncharacteristically ill at ease. "You caught that, did you?"

"I take it your cousin has a good sense of humor."

"Grady," Garrett said, as he slowly rubbed the back of his neck, "has a good sense of humor, all right."

Obviously he didn't want to explain. While as a youngster she'd have kept at him, pushed until she all but choked out the whole story, that wasn't appropriate now. They were two adult strangers whose lives had moved on from each other. People were entitled to their privacy. Goodness only knew, she hoped he'd respect hers.

"I don't think I want to hear about it," she said with a teasing lilt, letting him off the hook as she opened the door and climbed out.

In a twinkling he was at the side of the truck, probably grateful for the reprieve, and lifting out the toboggan. He set it on the ground, then snagged several bags and placed them atop it. Pulling two more from the bed of the truck, he handed her one and gripped the heavier of the two in his own hand.

"Ready?" Garrett grabbed the toboggan's tow rope. "Lead on."

With the side porch light illuminating the way, they progressed through the snow and up to the porch itself. Garrett held open the screen door as she fumbled with the keys to unlock the dead bolt. Then she stepped inside the dimly lit mudroom.

Ah, the infamous mudroom. Scene of the crime. Or rather the not-so-romantic setting of their first—and only—kiss.

The tiny space had been dark that night, too, an unexpected cocoon of privacy in a cabin teeming with family and friends readying for the Christmas Eve service. Now she self-consciously set the bag and backpack on a counter—the same counter she'd leaned against for support when her legs threatened to give way as Garrett's lips tentatively touched hers. Or tentatively at first, anyway.

Taking a quick breath, she flipped on the light switch, the bare bulb overhead banishing both the shadows and too-vivid memory. Avoiding meeting Garrett's gaze—afraid his own memories might have followed hers—she returned to the door and took the proffered bag.

He quickly transferred the remaining ones to the mudroom floor, then propped up the toboggan outside the door. "Looks like that about does it."

"Thanks, Garrett. I'll put the sled in the shed later." She slipped out of the old coat and hung it on a peg of the knotty pine–walled room. "Would you like to come in for a cup of cocoa? Or I could fix coffee."

In all honesty, she didn't want to invite him in. The less she saw of Garrett or any other old acquaintances during her brief stay here, the better. She needed time alone to work through things— the aching loss of Anton's recent death—and to make decisions for her professional future. Time to privately commemorate the loss of an unborn life. This use-it-or-lose-it vacation forced on her at the end of the year couldn't be better timed.

But the introspective hours she craved could too easily be aborted if she didn't guard them closely.

"Thanks for the invitation, but I have to get back to…" His uncertain gaze darted to hers as his voice trailed off.

What was with him tonight? Garrett in his youth had never been one to act unsure of himself or beat around the bush. "Get back to what? Your female fan club?"

Everything used to come easy to him. Athletics, schoolwork, making friends—and *girlfriends*. She used to give him a hard time about the latter, masking her own supersized crush.

His mouth twitched. "Believe me, no fan club these days. Actually, I need to get back to the church."

"Picking up another load of wood for delivery?"

"Not exactly." He cast a look upward as if appealing to the Heavenly realms. "I have to finish my sermon for tomorrow."

"Sermon?" She laughed, Grady's remark finally making sense. "You got roped into delivering a message at the old family church, didn't you? Garrett, whatever were you thinking?"

He ducked his head slightly, then looked up at her with one eye squinted. "I'm thinking that as the pastor of Christ's Church of Hunter Ridge, that's one of my responsibilities."

What? "Come on, tell me another one."

A smile tugged at the corners of his mouth. "As impossible as it may sound—and believe me, some days it probably seems more impossible to me than it does to you—I'm degreed in church ministry and have been interim pastor here for the past year."

She stared. He wasn't joking. His cousin hadn't been joking.

"Wow, Garrett."

He chuckled, no doubt in reaction to the stunned look on her face. "Yeah, wow."

"This is…is quite a stretch. I mean," she quickly amended, "a turnaround."

As they'd progressed from Sunday school days to youth group teen years, he'd become increasingly restless, adventurous, more prone to risk-taking. A party boy who'd enthusiastically indulged a wild streak, he'd certainly never anchored himself to anything spiritual, let alone God.

But then, she couldn't exactly point fingers…

"Which goes to prove—" his smile widened "—that God's still in the business of transforming lives."

"When did— How?" She never would have expected anything like this. Not in a million years.

He shrugged. "Looking back, God's been dogging me at least since my first rafting trip on the

Colorado when He really opened my eyes to the beauty and intricacy of His creation. Unfortunately, I wasn't willing to listen until about five years ago."

He was serious. This was for real.

"I'm sorry I laughed, Garrett. I was just so—"

"Shocked? Don't feel bad. My family, except for Mom and Grandma Jo, still isn't quite sure what to make of it. Some church members who knew 'the me that was' haven't bought into it, either."

She couldn't help but continue to stare at him. "This is amazing."

"That it is." He took a step back. "As usual, though, time's gotten away from me this week and my Sunday message awaits. But maybe we could get together while you're in town. Catch up."

She didn't want to catch *anybody* up on her life outside Hunter Ridge. Things she wasn't proud of. Wounds that had yet to heal. A faith that was currently so wobbly it wasn't funny. "Let's see how it goes, okay? There's lots to do to get this place ready to sell."

"You'll be at the worship service tomorrow?"

Not eager to interact with those who might remember her—or to see young mothers with their precious little ones—she hadn't planned to go. But having laughed at him, expressed such blatant disbelief, might Garrett take a refusal the wrong way?

"You can count on it."

"See you there then." Eyes smiling, he lifted his hand in a parting wave as he stepped off the side porch. "Ten thirty."

A few strides away, he halted in his tracks as if he'd thought of something he'd forgotten to say. Maybe he wanted to offer her a ride to church? Then apparently changing his mind, he tramped on through the falling snow.

Almost dazed, she stood at the door watching as he disappeared into the darkness. *Garrett McCrae. A pastor.* A heavy weight settled into the region of her heart as she closed and bolted the door.

Sorry to point this out, Lord, but your timing stinks.

She'd barely turned off the porch light and entered the kitchen when the door rattled from a firm pounding knock.

When she turned on the light and reopened the door, there stood Garrett once again.

"What did you forget?"

"Actually…" He paused as though undecided as to how to proceed. Totally un-Garrett-like. Then he plunged on. "I need to ask you something."

Oh, please, don't say anything about that night.

The night he'd made it clear his little tomboy pal didn't meet his standards for female companionship.

"I know you have to get this place cleaned up, but what if I helped? Recruited others to help?" His gaze now met hers in open appeal. "Do you think, then, that you might have time to oversee a church Christmas project while you're here?"

Was he kidding?

"I don't think there's much left to do," he hurried on, "but my office assistant who stays on top of it all year had a family emergency and can't follow through. All afternoon I beat the bushes to find a replacement, but came up empty-handed. Unless things have changed, though, you have more organizational ability in your little finger than most have in their whole body."

He gazed at her with hopeful eyes as she tried to make sense of what he was saying.

"You want me to take on a church project while I'm here?"

"Oversee it. You wouldn't have to do *all* the work. I imagine Melody has it well in hand. But none of the other volunteers feel confident in assuming the responsibility."

"To be honest, Garrett, I don't think I would either." No way did she want to be sucked into something like that, even for a good cause. Getting through church tomorrow would be about as much socializing as she could manage.

"You sell yourself short, Jodi." Garrett's words lilted persuasively, too reminiscent of times he'd conned her as a kid into doing things she'd later come to regret. "Remember how you turned around your Grandma's floundering yard sale? And you were only what—eleven? Twelve?"

"Thirteen." Grandma hadn't a clue about grouping similar items and showing them off to best advantage. Or about negotiation. Despite a clearly stickered, more-than-fair price, she would accept the first ridiculously low offer without batting an eye. In addition to rearranging the merchandise, Jodi had put a stop to that.

She couldn't help but smile at the memory.

"See?" Garrett almost gloated. "You *do* remember. You have a gift, Jodi, and maybe God's called you to be in town right now so you can use it for His glory."

She folded her arms. "I'm not falling for the 'God loves you and Garrett McCrae has a wonderful plan for your life' stuff."

Eyes twinkling, he shrugged. "Figured it was worth a try. So how about it? It won't take that much time, and I can round up some high schoolers to help whip your cabin into shape. Even if I have to get my own hands dirty, I'll see that you have extra time for the Christmas project. It's one that is near and dear to my Grandma Jo's heart—and was to your grandma's as well."

While help cleaning out the place would be welcome, no fair bringing Grandma into the equation.

"What exactly will this entail?" Why was she even asking, allowing Garrett to sway her after all these years? But maybe she *was* letting her personal problems turn her into a Grinch as her sisters had accused. Becoming selfish. *All about me.* "I'd be organizing the distribution of canned goods? Clothing? Toys?"

"All of the above. Behind-the-scenes work."

Would it really kill her to help out? To make a little room in her own plans during the next two weeks? She might not be able to boil water, but she did have a knack for project management, a talent she was paid well for in the corporate world. How hard could it be if this Melody person had been keeping on top of the project since early in the year as Garrett claimed? And maybe it would be a means of honoring her grandmother's memory.

"I guess… I can take this on."

Garrett grinned. "You won't regret it, Jodi, I promise. Melody says this project is the highlight of her whole year—that there's nothing better for the soul than making the holiday season brighter for unwed mothers."

A blast of cold air from the open door swirled in around Jodi's ankles, sending a shiver rippling through her.

Unwed mothers?

"You'd better get moving, Garrett. You don't want to be late again."

Cutting off his hummed rendition of "O Holy Night," he glanced at the rail-thin gray-haired woman standing in the doorway to his room on Sunday morning. Seventy-year-old Dolly Lovell and her husband had taken him in as a boarder a year ago when he'd been cautioned that as a single pastor it might not be advisable to get a place of his own and he hadn't want to bunk back with his folks. As it turned out, this lodging arrangement not only came with meals and occasional help with laundry, but also built-in chaperones.

"I'm heading out right now." He reached to the top of an antique dresser for his Bible and an iPad filled with sermon notes, then gave his part-time church receptionist a kiss on the cheek. "I don't know what I'd do without you and Al to keep me on the straight and narrow."

Dressed for church herself, a smiling Dolly shook her head as he slipped by her. "It's a dirty job, Pastor McCrae, but somebody has to do it."

There was probably more truth in her humorous comment than he cared to think about. Born with—and long indulging—an independent streak made coming under the authority of the church leadership a never-ending challenge. Both for him *and* them.

It wasn't far to the church, a distance he most often enjoyed walking, but this morning he jumped in his old Ford Explorer to make better time. Although he didn't have a Sunday school class to teach this quarter—he'd used the extra hour this morning to shovel out the Lovells' driveway and polish up his sermon—he'd caught his mind wandering one too many times. If he was late, it would be Jodi Thorpe's fault.

He could still hear her laughter when she thought Grady's preacher comment was a joke. Could see the shock in her eyes at his admission that he was an official God's man. He wasn't unaccustomed to that reaction since returning to Hunter Ridge, of course. With the exception of Drew, he'd taken a lot of ribbing from his high school buddies—and even was shunned by a few. Many adults who'd known him when he was growing up eyed him with skepticism. No surprise. But for some reason Jodi's disbelief pierced him to the core.

Admittedly, it *was* a stretch to accept the changes in his life. Especially when Jodi was standing in the mudroom where as a hormone-driven teen he'd once attempted to put the moves on her right under her family's nose. But deep down he'd hoped to hear the friend of his youth confess she'd seen something in his early years that foreshadowed this turn of events. Or that her grandmother had admitted to glimpsing a nugget of promise in him.

More likely, though, all her grandma saw was an undisciplined young rascal who couldn't keep his hands to himself.

Nevertheless, Jodi had agreed to take on this year's Christmas project. A load off his shoulders, for which he was grateful.

As always, his spirits rose at the sight of the church building. This morning the weathered brick edifice, built in the 1930s, looked like something out of a magazine with snow coating the roof and the surrounding ponderosa pines. Some noble soul had shoveled the walkways and bladed the parking lot, the sun now pitching in to do its part.

There were good people here at Christ's Church. He was more than fortunate to land a ministry opportunity with a congregation like this one as he prepared for a future in missions work. But did they consider themselves equally blessed to have been saddled with him? They'd been pretty desperate when he'd come along. Following the departure of their third minister in as many years, they'd been without one for six months when Grandma Jo took a hand in things.

And now they'd be looking for a replacement once again.

"Garrett!"

His cousin Luke Hunter—Grady's older brother—waved him over as he approached the front of the church. A newlywed of only a few months, he looked happier than he had in years. The high-spirited former Delaney Marks had certainly impacted the widower and father of three in a big way. He was much more relaxed now, less hardheaded, and occasionally could even pass for laid-back. While Garrett hadn't heard anything official, if Grandma Jo's suspicions were correct, child number four might be putting in an appearance not too far into next summer.

When he reached his relative's side, the men shook hands, and his cousin lowered his voice. "I want to give you a heads-up. Old Man Moppert isn't happy that you've rearranged things at the front of the church."

Randall Moppert. Again. The guy had never forgiven him for TP-ing his trees when, in the pitch dark and slightly inebriated, a teenage Garrett had mistaken Moppert's place for that of a friend next door.

"I didn't rearrange. I shifted the lectern and the

Lord's Supper table slightly off-center so there's room for the kids' choir. They're kicking off our service with 'Away in a Manger.'"

"Well, he doesn't like it. I overheard him telling one of the board members that you're taking liberties in God's house."

"I'll talk to him."

"Better you than me." Luke grimaced, then glanced with interest toward the parking lot. "Who's that with the Palmers?"

Following the trajectory of his cousin's gaze, Garrett's heart rate kicked up a notch at the sight of a pretty woman, her red-gold hair flowing around her shoulders as she exited a vehicle. The Palmers must have seen Jodi walking into town and picked her up.

Which was another thing nagging at him.

Last night he'd said he hoped to see her at church, but although grateful for her taking on the project and aware she didn't have transportation, he hadn't offered any.

The church where he'd done a semester's internship had strict guidelines on staff interactions with members of the opposite sex, and he'd instinctively maintained those standards as much as possible when he'd come to Hunter Ridge—even if their rules were more lenient. Which is why he hadn't accepted Jodi's invitation to join her inside for cocoa. But he could have at least drummed up a ride for her.

She looked amazing this morning, her fair cheeks rosy from the cold and a bright smile rivaling the warmth of the morning's welcome sun. Then there was that eye-catching, begging-to-be-touched long hair that as a kid her folks kept cropped up by her ears. Not for the first time, he whispered a silent prayer of thanks that she wouldn't be in town long. Although many times a partner in his schemes when they were kids, she'd increasingly balked when he took his risk-taking tendencies to the extreme. No doubt she'd be unsurprised that those inclinations had finally caught up with him—and he was paying the price.

"Garrett? I said—"

"That's Jodi Thorpe," Garrett quickly responded, his face warming at Luke's curious look. Had anyone else noticed him gaping at the newcomer? Not recommended ministerial manners. "She used to spend summers up here. Sometimes Thanksgiving or Christmas. You may not remember her. She'd have only been about seven or eight when you left for the military."

"Thanks for the reminder of my old age." Although still on the sunny side of forty with a wife ten years his junior, Luke gave him a mild look of reprimand. "I don't remember a Jodi, but I do remember the last name. Grandma Jo was good friends with a Nadene Thorpe. This is a granddaughter?"

"Right. Hey, look, I'll talk to you later, okay?" Maybe he could make amends for not arranging transportation for Jodi. "I'm going to welcome her to Christ's Church."

Luke leaned in. "You do that, *flirt master*, but don't forget you have a million eyes on you right now. Until you hear otherwise, you're still in the running for a full-time position here. Don't blow it."

Luke's warning was unnecessary. Not only did he have God looking over his shoulder, but he was acutely conscious of how closely a single pastor was watched—and judged. Good impressions were especially important right now, even though, unknown to those around him, he had no intention of staying in Hunter Ridge, job offer or no job offer.

"No worries," he assured Luke as his gaze drifted back to the subject in question. "As a kid, that gal over there could shinny up a tree faster than lightning and nail a can with a slingshot better than I could. She once caught me off guard and pinned me down, too. Filled my mouth with a handful of dirt. Believe me, recollections like that kinda put a damper on any flirting business."

Or they would, anyway, if he could forget how sweet it had been to kiss her.

Chapter Three

Jodi had barely drawn back from giving a big thank-you hug to Marisela Palmer—one of her grandma's dear friends—when Garrett approached.

Or rather, *Pastor* McCrae.

Unbelievable.

It was with a sense of relief, though, that the guy she'd known since the summer before first grade hadn't let himself be shoehorned into a suit for his Sunday morning duties. Rather, he had on a pair of neatly pressed gray trousers, a white collared shirt, and a gray pullover sweater. No outer jacket despite the chilly morning.

She couldn't resist firing the first volley. "What happened to your tie, Pastor?"

His hand flew to his neck as he looked frantically on the ground around him. "It was there a minute ago."

"I think Jodi's teasing you, Garrett. Just like old times." Marisela, a petite black woman who looked at least a decade younger than Jodi knew her to be, looped her arm through his as she gazed up at him with affection. "I spied her coming out of Nadene's cabin this morning—a delightful surprise—and we gave her a ride. She tells me she had no idea until last night that you've been our minister this past year."

He patted Marisela's hand, but his amused gaze held Jodi's. "It looks as if she sufficiently recovered from the shock since she managed to get herself here on time this morning."

Garrett *would* have to remember that Grandma practically had to dynamite her out of bed, and often she'd dragged herself to the breakfast table still in her pajamas.

Before Jodi could make a snappy response, a pretty brunette with two small children in tow paused next to Garrett. Bundled against the cold, the faux fur–trimmed hood of the woman's burgundy coat framed a heart-shaped face and long-lashed dark eyes. She looked up at him expectantly, as if assuming introductions would be made.

Jodi's heart jolted. His wife and kids? Right before turning off the bedside lamp last night, she'd realized Garrett hadn't clarified a marital status. But a quick glance at both his and the woman's ungloved—and ringless—hands put the question to rest. So Garrett *was* single and still playing the field, although aspects of that part of his life would certainly have made a U-turn, as well.

His gaze flickered to the newcomer. "Sofia, you know Marisela. But I'd like you to meet Jodi Thorpe. Our grandmothers were good friends. Jodi, this is Sofia Ramos and her daughter Tiana."

He placed a hand affectionately on the head of the black-haired little girl next to him. "Her little brother is Leon."

While early grade schooler Tiana smiled shyly, Leon, appearing to be about three, paid Jodi no attention as he tugged at his mother's coat, eager to be on his way.

"It's good to meet you." Jodi shook Sofia's offered hand.

"Are you visiting for the holidays, Jodi?"

"My folks are selling my grandparents' cabin, so I'm here to get it ready to put on the market." That response seemed to satisfy everyone.

"Such a shame to sell the place." Marisela shook her head. "But while they keep the utilities turned on and things in good repair, your folks haven't been up here at all this year."

Garrett looked down at his watch and made a face.

"Oops. Showtime. Children's choir has the opening number." He held out a hand to each child. "Kiddos? Let's get you in there for your moment in the spotlight—all set for your mama's ever-ready camera if she can sneak off the piano bench for a few shots."

Both giggling children willingly grasped a hand and trotted up the front steps beside him, evidently comfortable in the man's presence. Which again made Jodi wonder about his relationship with their mother.

Mr. and Mrs. Palmer invited her to sit with them, and it was with a mix of nostalgia and a sense of time too quickly passing that she spied a few now-older yet familiar faces—including Garrett's spunky Grandma Jo, who came over to warmly welcome her.

Much of the service was a blur as youthful memories assailed. Sunshine streaming through the stained glass windows illuminated the red velvet bows on each pew, and the familiar scent of furniture oil tickled memories. Remembrances of squirming on a hard pew at her grandmother's side vividly filled her mind, as did later instances of covertly watching a restless, teenage Garrett sitting with his buddies.

It all blended together with Sofia's lovely piano renditions in the background, that is until Garrett stood to deliver the morning's message. As if he had a direct hotline to her troubled soul, his words regarding right and wrong choices—how split-second decisions could make a lasting impact—unexpectedly hit their fragile target.

It was all she could do to maintain her composure as a montage of uncomfortable images flashed through her mind. Her life was such a muddled mess right now, mostly due to choices made. God had forgiven her. She believed that, not because she *felt* forgiven, but because that's what He promised. But hadn't she also paid for her mistakes in the worst possible way?

Now she'd very likely lose her job, too, through no fault of her own. Was it any wonder her faith was tottering? She took a steadying breath as a too-familiar suffocating sensation pressed in.

"Jodi? Would you like to join us?"

Jerked back to the present, she realized the service had concluded. She'd zoned out through the closing hymn, people were milling in the aisles, and Marisela was standing beside her, smiling uncertainly.

She gave an apologetic laugh as she stood to slip back into her jacket. "I'm sorry, I didn't catch that. Join you where?"

"Al and Dolly Lovell have invited us to lunch. You remember Dolly, don't you? Another of your grandmother's friends? You're invited, too—or we'd be happy to drop you off at the cabin if you'd prefer."

"Oh, do come." Another older woman, her fair

hair cut in a chin-length bob, placed a hand on her arm. "You remember me, don't you? Georgia Gates. I was your vacation Bible school teacher in third and fourth grades. Your grandma was such a dear friend. We miss her so much."

"Of course, I remember you." But for a fleeting moment, surrounded by those who knew and loved Nadene Thorpe, she couldn't help but wonder why Grandma couldn't still be there among them, too.

While she'd prefer to return to the seclusion of the cabin, she didn't want to be rude to her grandma's friends. If she got through the expected socializing today, she could then oversee the Christmas project as quickly and efficiently as possible. After that, she'd be free to withdraw from human contact for the remainder of her time in Hunter Ridge. "I'd be delighted to come as long as I won't be intruding."

"Of course you won't be," Georgia said, giving her arm a squeeze. "We'd love to catch up on your life and that of your folks and sisters."

Thankfully, they could all reminisce about Grandma, too, and there was plenty she could fill them in on regarding family members—marriages, kids, travels. She should be able to keep the attention off herself for the most part.

She'd started down the main aisle when she caught a glimpse of a familiar-looking young man in a wheelchair making his way toward a nearby side door she knew led to an outside ramp. She paused as her grandmother's friends continued toward the back of the church.

Drew Everton?

He'd been one of her friends from church and a longtime buddy of Garrett's. Top-notch student. Athlete extraordinaire. But she didn't see any sign of a cast or elevated leg, so what had…? He glanced up and caught her eye, an ear-to-ear grin illuminating his face. Then he expertly spun the wheelchair in her direction.

"Well, look who's here." His eyes smiled as he rolled up to her. "My mom said she thought she saw you, but I didn't believe her."

"Moms are always to be believed. It's me."

"You look great, Jodi." His dark-eyed gaze warmed as he looked her over. "Better than great."

"Thanks. You do, too." A lock of sand-colored hair dipping over his forehead, he was even better-looking than she remembered from the last time she'd seen him when he was a senior in high school. He'd sometimes joined her and Garrett in their youthful escapades, but he didn't have that wild streak Garrett had been known for. He'd been more cautious, a look-before-you-leap sort, a steadying influence that probably kept Garrett out of more serious trouble. "How *are* you, Drew?"

He gave a self-deprecating laugh and motioned to his legs. "I do all right, considering I can no longer chase after cute little gals like you and can't outrun their boyfriends should I attempt to steal a kiss."

She smiled uncertainly. "What happened?"

He shrugged. "A little accident. You think you're in control of your life and the next thing you know, you get your legs knocked out from under you. In my case, literally."

"This is…permanent?"

"It's been my reality for several years, but who's to say? Strides are being made in medical science, and God can always choose to step in. So I'm not giving up hope."

"I admire your attitude, but I'm sorry, Drew. This can't be easy."

A shadow flickered through his eyes. "Far from that."

His attention was caught by something behind her and his expression brightened. "Hey, you! Get on over here before I make off with your pretty little buddy."

She turned as Garrett approached. He nodded to her, and the two men shook hands.

"Did you know Jodi was in town?" Drew studied his friend intently. "You kept that to yourself."

Garrett raised his hands in a gesture of innocence. "I only found out last night. Ran into her by accident."

Drew squinted one eye. "That true, Jodi?"

"One hundred percent." It seemed surreal to be standing here talking to these two grown men she'd known when they were boys, and again she felt that faint sensation of suffocation. Disorientation. "I'll be in town long enough to take care of family business related to Grandma and Grandpa's cabin and then right back out again."

"Maybe we can—"

"Wish I could let you two catch up on old times." Garrett gave them a regretful look. "But Marisela Palmer sent me in here to retrieve Jodi, and I don't want her to come looking for the both of us."

"Scaredy-cat," Drew taunted.

"Guilty as charged." He tilted his head toward Jodi. "Marisela's in the car and waiting."

She and Drew said their goodbyes, then she impulsively leaned over to give him a quick hug.

"Talk about a shock," she whispered to Garrett as they stepped into the noontime sun and still-crisp air. "I feel so bad for Drew."

Garrett's jaw hardened as he nodded, but he didn't meet her gaze. "Me, too."

"How did you con this poor girl into taking on the Christmas project, Garrett? Shame on you for

burdening a visitor with church responsibilities."
Georgia Gates clucked her tongue as she gazed at
him from across the Lovells' dining table. "When
we heard Melody headed off to Texas, we thought
for sure you'd recruit Sofia."

Here we go again.

Garrett reluctantly looked up from his half-
eaten apple pie to focus his attention on the older
woman. Aware that all eyes at the Sunday lunch
table were on him—including Jodi's—he placed
his fork on his plate and carefully schooled his
features to what he hoped was a pastor-like de-
meanor.

The ink had barely dried on his church contract when it seemed a not-too-subtle campaign
commenced to set him up with Sofia Ramos. Is
that why all the church ladies he'd talked to yesterday turned down his plea for assistance? They
thought if none of them stepped up he'd be forced
to call on the attractive single mom?

But they didn't know Sofia's whole story, and
it wasn't his to tell.

"I think Sofia's hands are plenty full right now,
don't you, Georgia? She's working full-time, and
there are Leon's health issues to consider."

"I've always heard," Georgia persisted, with
an emphatic nod to the others, "that if you need
something done, give it to the person who is al-

ready successfully juggling a million things and they'll get it done, too. That's our Sofia."

"It's the holidays, though." Garrett again picked up his fork. "Let's show her a little mercy, shall we?"

Jodi gave him a pointed look as if to convey he hadn't let *her* off the hook for the holidays. But Sofia was the widow of a volunteer fireman who'd been killed on an icy winter road two years ago. She had enough on her shoulders as it was.

"The issue's been settled, Georgia," Dolly chimed in, coming to his rescue. "Thanks to Jodi, who has a big heart like her dear grandma."

Marisela smiled at Jodi fondly. "You probably wouldn't remember—you were only here a few days at Christmas some years—but your grandmother had so much fun helping Melody make deliveries. She loved holding the babies."

"So, then, young lady—" Good-natured Bert Palmer, Marisela's balding, rotund husband, leaned a forearm on the table. "Christmas is two weeks away. What's the plan?"

Startled—and looking prettier in that emerald-green turtleneck sweater than a woman had a right to look—Jodi's gaze flew to Garrett. "I assumed that at some point that's what someone would tell *me*."

"She accepted the role last night, Bert." Garrett set his fork down again with an inward sigh. Forget the pie. "I picked up Melody's notes and checklist from the office this morning, so we need time to sort it out."

"You'll need volunteers. I can help." Georgia smiled encouragingly at Jodi. Then, apparently realizing she'd been asked to volunteer yesterday and turned him down flat, she cut a sheepish look in Garrett's direction. "I can help, Pastor. But I can't take on the whole thing right now. Getting ready for grandkids coming next week, you know."

"I can assist, too." Marisela nodded in Jodi's direction. "I've helped in past years but, like Georgia, I couldn't assume responsibility for it all."

Dolly cut another slice of pie and slid it onto her husband's offered plate. "You can count on me, too, sweetheart. Let me know what I need to do. The young unwed mothers are so appreciative of any assistance they get, and we always come through for them. Baby food. Diapers. Maternity and infant wear. All topped off by a generous helping of things intended to pamper them a bit. I love seeing their faces when they open the packages."

Jodi's gaze, unexpectedly bleak, met Garrett's.

Guilt stabbed. Had he, in trying to get the project off his own overloaded plate, asked her to take on too much?

* * *

Unwed mothers.

She still couldn't believe she'd signed on to immerse herself in the world of young women with babies and no husbands. That was a situation she could all too vividly relate to. But she'd given Garrett her word, and Grandma's friends were looking at her as if she were Grandma come back to life.

But Garrett now appeared rather uncertain. Was he having second thoughts about her ability to take it on, thinking she'd let him and the church down?

Despite the initial shock last night, she could handle this. There was no reason she had to spend time *with* unwed mothers and their infants, was there? She'd sit in the overseer's chair and delegate. Her grandmother's friends promised support, as, she assumed, would others. They could be the ones making any required personal contacts.

Holding the babies.

Feeling the phone vibrating in the purse nestled by her feet, she excused herself from the table. In the hallway outside the dining room, she checked the caller ID. Her sister, Star.

"Aunt Jodi?" The giggling voice of her sister's five-year-old, Bethany, came through the earpiece.

"Hi, sweetie."

"Is it true you're a Grinch?" A peal of childish laughter ensued, and Jodi could hear Star whispering something to her daughter as she took possession of the phone.

"Funny, Star."

"I didn't coach her to say that, Jodi. Honest."

"Maybe not. But she overheard that somewhere, and I doubt the source is your ever-lovin' husband."

"Well, if the shoe fits…"

"It doesn't."

"The kids are disappointed that you aren't coming here for Christmas. They were looking forward to you taking them to see the holiday lights at the Phoenix Zoo again this year."

She'd miss that, too. The zoo put on a display of almost four million lights, special shows and rides to delight kids of all ages. Even grown-up ones.

"The thing is, things are really up in the air right now with my job and other stuff, and I told Mom and Dad I'd get the cabin in shape to put on the market while they're in Mexico."

"Which brings me to the reason I called. We're not going to let you spend Christmas all by yourself. Ronda and I and the kids are coming up a couple of days before Christmas."

Her heart sank.

"Isn't that a great idea?" Her sister's voice rose

in excited anticipation. "Our hubbies will join us Christmas Eve."

This could not be happening. Not now. Not when she needed time alone. Time to ask God some hard questions and, hopefully, get her life back on track.

"Star, this isn't a good idea. I'm here a limited amount of time to get the cabin in shape. I can't do that with a houseful of kids underfoot." While Star's Bethany could be counted on to behave herself, little sister Savannah was only three and would be at that better-watch-her-every-minute stage. Then there was sister Ronda's four-year-old, Henry, who, from what she'd been told, was still a rambunctious handful.

"We can help," Star continued. "The kids will play outside most of the time, especially if it snows. You do have snow already, don't you? I think I saw that on the news."

"Yes, there's snow, but—"

"Perfect. They can go sledding and build snowmen like we used to do. And what was that game we played with the paths made in the snow? Fox and geese or something like that?"

"Yes, but—"

"Ronda and I were reminiscing last night about all the wonderful times we had at our grandparents' place up there. Amazing summers and fun-filled Christmases. Stringing popcorn for the big tree. Opening grab-bag presents. Finding baby Jesus in the manger on Christmas morning. Remember?" She sighed happily. "We were so fortunate to experience that—something our kids have never gotten to enjoy. Something that they'll never have the opportunity to experience when the cabin sells."

"Star—"

"This is it, Jodi, our last chance." Her sister's voice now openly pleaded. "I know you can pull something amazing together for the kids' sake. Our last big Christmas together at the cabin. One like Grandma and Grandpa used to give us."

Would kids that young actually make any lasting memories from a family get-together at the cabin—or was this a front for her sisters' own nostalgic journey?

Still trying to take in all her sister was saying, Jodi stared blankly down the hallway, then caught movement out of the corner of her eye—Garrett, who'd stepped to the dining room door, his eyes filled with concern.

"Everything okay?" he mouthed.

Oh, sure. Everything was fine. *Just fine.*

Chapter Four

"Thanks again, Garrett, for the loan of the pickup."

Jodi's words warmed him as he sat across from her in a cozy corner of his book-lined church office Monday morning, the soft strains of "Joy to the World" wafting from the open door that led to his now-absent assistant's work area, manned today by Dolly.

The grateful smile of his childhood friend was enough to tempt even the most determined man to rethink his priorities. But being tempted and following through on temptation were two different matters. He'd committed to a plan for his future, and not even Jodi reappearing in his life could stop him now.

Besides, undoubtedly she still thought of him as a big brother. She had no idea how he couldn't get her out of his mind for months after that amazing kiss he'd recklessly drawn her into. How he'd tried to shrug it off. Joke it off. Run other guys off. He'd never forget, either, the shock in her eyes. Big brothers didn't kiss little sisters like that. He'd broken a trust.

Did she think, by his asking her to help on the church project, that he still had designs on her? If so, no wonder she'd looked dazed after he'd all but twisted her arm to "volunteer."

"Rio's more than happy to lend you her truck since she's out of town until Christmas." Having Jodi on foot would have been problematic, but driving her around town and to neighboring communities could only lead to being targets of gossip. So he'd gotten in touch with his cousin Rio—Grady and Luke's little sister—and found a solution.

Jodi shook her head as if in wonder, the burgundy shade of a cable-knit sweater lending an attractive glow to her fair skin. "It's so funny to think Rio's all grown up now. I remember when she was competing at the county fair kids' barrel-racing division in elementary school."

"Twenty-one next spring and still barrel racing."

"Makes me feel old." A shadow that troubled him flickered momentarily through her eyes as she shifted in the wingback chair to look out the window beside them. Rio's red pickup, parked in the gravel back lot next to his SUV, already sported a light layer of snow. It looked like the lingering effects of an El Niño weather pattern were going to make themselves known this winter.

She again turned her attention to him, holding up the compact spiral notebook in which she'd been writing as they'd talked. "It sounds as though there's still a lot to be done."

In the past hour, they'd gone over the budget and checklist, and brainstormed strategies— over which they had opposing ideas—to meet the looming deadline. Not counting today, there were only eleven days until everything had to be delivered before Christmas Eve. Had his powerhouse office assistant actually thought it could be pulled together in such a short time?

Now he'd unintentionally dumped his own headache on Jodi.

"I apologize for that. Melody's usually on top of things. One of the most organized people I know, and she keeps me organized, too. But with her mother passing away last spring and then trying to keep tabs on her father's welfare from a distance, I don't think her focus was on the project as it usually is much of the year."

"There's a lot of solicitation yet to be done for both monetary and physical item donation. Then supplementary purchases to be made. And distribution."

"That sums it up." He ran his hand through his

hair. "You know, though, Jodi, like I said yesterday when you told me about your family coming, you don't have to do this. It's certainly a worthwhile project to help out unwed moms in the area, but Georgia was right. This isn't your responsibility. Church members need to pick up the ball and run with it."

Or *he'd* have to.

He couldn't risk a dark blot on his performance evaluation right here at the end of the year should the annual Christmas project flop. But he'd do all he could not to call on Sofia. Neither of them needed to encourage the matchmakers.

"Grandma's friends said they'd help." Jodi's chin lifted as she offered a determined smile, reminiscent of childhood days when she'd set her mind to something. "I'll make getting funding and donation commitments a priority this week, then leave it to the others if it comes down to that."

He squinted one eye. "From what you shared with me this morning, though, this is the first real vacation you've had all year. Maybe in several years."

"I'm good with it." She tapped the notebook now on her lap. "I have Melody's cell number, checklist and contact numbers of past donors. I can take it from here."

It sounded as if she wanted him to stay out

of the way. Why should that disappoint him? Wasn't that what he wanted—someone else to take over the project and free up his time for other demands?

"Okay, then, if you're sure." He stood to look down at her, noticing how her hair glinted softly in the lamplight. "Did you want to take a look at the storeroom? See what has already come in?"

"Good idea."

She'd just risen to her feet, standing what some might consider a shade too close, when Sofia appeared in the doorway, a plate of cookies clutched in her hands.

"Oh, I'm sorry." Her dark-lashed eyes widened slightly. "I didn't know you had someone with you. Whoever is covering for Melody today must have stepped away."

She motioned apologetically to the work area behind her.

"We're finishing up." He took a step back, putting more distance between him and Jodi. "I'm going to show Jodi the storeroom where we keep donations for the unwed mothers project. She's going to manage it while Melody's away."

"Oh, really? When I heard yesterday that Melody had to leave town abruptly, I thought for sure I'd hear from you with a plea for assistance." Sofia thrust the plate of cookies into his hands— pumpkin spice, his favorite—then focused a curious gaze on Jodi. "That's very…nice of you, especially considering you're only in town for a short time."

"Blackmailed," Jodi whispered in a deliberately audible aside. "Believe me, someone who has known you since you were a first grader has loads of ammunition to work with."

She cut a playful look at him.

"Come on now, don't give Sofia the impression I railroaded you into this."

"You didn't?"

He had. Sort of. But he'd given her the opportunity to back out, hadn't he? "You said you could handle it."

"And I can." She leaned toward Sofia, mischief still in her eyes. "Garrett and I don't quite see eye to eye on some of the details, so you'd be doing me a great service if you could keep him out from underfoot."

"I think that can be arranged." Sofia's own gaze now teased as she looked up at him.

"Well, then—" Suddenly feeling compelled to escape the confines of the small office, he set the cookies on his desk, then motioned them both toward the door. "Please join us, Sofia."

No way did he want anyone stumbling across him alone in a storage room with Jodi. Where was Dolly when he needed her?

Together they made their way to the wing of

the church that housed classrooms and a fellowship hall. In a side hallway, he unlocked a door
with a smiling paper snowman taped to it. Then,
holding it open to reveal a shadowed, eight-by-
twelve shelved space, he flipped on the light.

It was all he could do not to gasp aloud.

Viewing the sole package of disposable diapers
sitting on the floor, Sofia looked at him doubtfully. "The cupboard looks pretty bare, Garrett."

Where did everything go?

"Melody took some stuff to the crisis pregnancy center in Canyon Springs earlier in the fall,
but it looks as if it hasn't been replenished." As
pastor of the church, he should have been more
attuned, not let it fall through the cracks. But he'd
trusted his office assistant. Last December when
he'd started here, the room had been overflowing
with holiday baby bounty even before the final
push for donations.

"We'll get this room filled," Jodi said matter-
of-factly as she stepped away from the door, but
not meeting his likely guilt-filled gaze. She probably wanted to throttle him. But he'd always been
able to count on her to come through for him
when they were kids. Covering for him. Saving
him from the repercussions of his own misdeeds
and shortcomings.

Apparently, despite the rough-and-tumble tomboy's transformation in many other ways, that invaluable attribute hadn't changed.

He took a relieved breath.

God rest ye merry gentlemen, let nothing you dismay...

"I'm sorry to hear that, Mr. Bealer."

Jodi stared blankly across the room at the cabin's stone fireplace, the phone pressed to her ear. Pete Bealer was the seventh person on Melody's contact list that she'd called following the "enlightening" meeting with Garrett. At the rate things were going, she'd consider herself fortunate to have a single baby rattle to split among the unwed mothers next week. Oh, and that package of disposable diapers sitting in the otherwise empty storage room.

"Wish I could help out but, yeah, it's been a rough year," the owner of the local ice-cream shop continued. "As much as I'd like to, I can't even blame all those artists in town for this one. According to the Chamber of Commerce's findings, they actually drew even more business to Hunter Ridge last summer than the one before. Go figure."

He chuckled. It was nice he could find humor in the fact that his outgo had nearly exceeded his income.

"I heard it was unusually cool late in the summer," she commiserated.

"It was, it was. Near-record rainfall, too. So folks were looking for something to warm them up rather than cool them down. I hear eateries with a fireplace or woodstove did a booming business."

"Well, thank you for your time. I hope things go better for you next year."

She returned the cell phone to her purse, then surveyed the knotty pine–walled, open-plan space—living room, kitchen, dining area—remembering it as much bigger than it was in actuality. Yes, there were two small bedrooms and an attic room that stretched the length of the cabin, but how had Grandma and Grandpa packed them all in here when Mom and Dad, her sisters, and other friends and relatives gathered for a weekend or longer?

It had been a comfy, kid-friendly retreat, with two sofas and several rockers. Folding card tables leaned against the wall for playing games at night. A bookcase filled with classics had welcomed them on a rainy day. And next week the now-silent rooms would be filled once again. But how did her sisters expect her to replicate for their children the delightful Christmases they remembered?

She wasn't Grandma.

A touch of melancholy permeated as she moved to the front window to watch snow flurries dancing through the early-afternoon air. Maybe her sisters were right. She *was* becoming a Grinch. And so much for the phone calls she'd made, trying to drum up a bit of Christmas spirit among potential donors—and within herself. An hour's worth of effort down the drain when she had too many other things to attend to.

"Where," she mumbled aloud, "is all the good cheer and generosity characteristic of the season?" No doubt she'd have had more success with her calls two weeks ago, before credit card bills from Black Friday purchases started rolling in.

She glanced over at the stack of Christmas decoration boxes she'd dragged out of the attic last night, but hadn't the heart to open. It hadn't been her intention to decorate during the brief time she was in town, but with her nieces and nephew coming next week and her sisters anticipating a nostalgic sojourn to the good old days, they clearly expected a little effort on her part.

Maybe if she wasn't trying to manage the church project, clean the cabin *and* prayerfully sort through her tumultuous life, she could handle a little holiday festivity for the kids. Maybe. Playing hostess wasn't one of her God-given gifts.

"How did I get myself into this?" Her voice reverberated through the raftered, wood-floored space.

No thundering voice from Heaven responded to her plaintive query. But then she already knew the answer to how she'd gotten saddled with the Christmas project—and unwed mothers of all things. It came down to the unfortunate fact that she was still infatuated with Garrett McCrae. Dumb. Dumb. Dumb. She was too old for crushes, especially on someone who'd made it clear that kissing her had been the worst mistake of his life.

Are you kidding me? Kissing Jodi would be about as thrilling as kissing our Labrador retriever. And she'd probably double up her fist and belt the first guy who tried.

Her breath caught at the still-vivid memory. After a heart-soaring kiss only a short while earlier, she'd overheard him joking with his buddies later that same night, after the Christmas Eve service. One of them—Richard?—had mumbled something she didn't catch, and Garrett's mocking response brought a round of laughter that she could still hear. Could still feel the hot waves of humiliation that had coursed through her.

Thankfully, neither Garrett nor any of the others had seen her, and shaking all the way to her core, she'd slipped silently away. But it cut deep, making it the worst Christmas of her whole life. The worst, that is, until she lost a baby to miscarriage four years ago this very month.

Looking back now, she recognized that she'd allowed overhearing Garrett and the laughter of the other boys to set her up for a fall when, not too many years later, Kel O'Connor blarneyed her—and her rickety self-image—right into his arms and into his bed.

Jodi clenched her fists. She was *not* going to think about Kel right now. Or Garrett. Not even Anton, although he was an innocent party in all of this.

As she took a step away from the window, she glimpsed an SUV making its way up the pine-lined lane to the cabin. Garrett. What was he doing here? He hadn't said anything about stopping by.

There was someone in the seat beside him, too. Sofia? No, thankfully it was Dolly. Sofia, although seemingly as sweet as could be, was one of those women who made her overly aware of her own shortcomings in the domesticity department. Those cookies she'd delivered while Jodi was at the church hadn't looked store-bought, but what exactly was her relationship with Garrett that she was stopping by his office in the middle of the morning? Hadn't he mentioned on Sunday that she worked someplace full-time?

"This is a surprise," Jodi said as she ushered her guests in from the cold.

"I told Dolly about the bargain I'd made with you." Garrett unlooped what looked to be a hand-crocheted scarf from around his neck—Sofia's work?—and hung it on the coatrack by the door. His jacket joined it. "You know, how if you helped with the Christmas project, I'd see that you got assistance cleaning this place."

"He bullied you into cleaning, Dolly?" Jodi gave Garrett a look of reprimand as he helped the older woman off with her coat. He'd said earlier that he'd have high schoolers pitch in, not drag one of her grandma's friends into it.

"In case you haven't noticed, he's more of a sweet-talker than a bully. Which is why we've been delighted to have him heading up Christ's Church's ministry." His landlady smiled at him with affection in her eyes. "I told him I'd be happy to help, and he suggested we find out firsthand exactly what you need to have done."

"Well…" Jodi looked around the space somewhat helplessly. A housekeeper came in once a week in Philly while she was at work, so she wasn't certain what all might be involved in that vaguely mysterious process. Kind of like the baffling nuances of home cooking—that's what delis and restaurant takeout were for, right? "Mom and Dad haven't been here this year, so everything's dusty. And they said they haven't done deep cleaning in years. I've found more than a few cobwebs."

Which she was *not* touching.

"Cobwebs?" Garrett's eyes gleamed. "That must have made your day."

"Funny." She gave him a smirk, then offered an explanation to Dolly. "When we were kids Garrett talked me into going first when we were exploring one of the attic spaces under the eaves, knowing full well spiders had strung their sticky webs across our intended path."

She shuddered at the memory, and Garrett laughed.

"That's our Garrett." Dolly shook her head in amusement. "Is it okay, Jodi, if I take a look around? That will give me an idea of what type of cleaning supplies I need to bring."

"Look to your heart's content. And I'll pay for any supplies."

Dolly disappeared in the direction of the bedrooms and bath. *One* bathroom. How on earth would her family get through next week in a packed house?

Garrett clapped his hands together. "So, how's it going with the project? Have you drummed up any donations?"

Jodi rubbed her hands up and down her sweatered arms to warm herself up. Another thing she'd need to get—firewood. "I made a few calls with little to show for it."

As in nothing.

"I plan to hit it hard this afternoon," she continued, unwilling to admit defeat. "But I may call Melody first. See if she has any tips."

"I remember her saying that some years she'd get more of one thing than another and had to fill in for what came up short."

This year might take a *lot* of supplementing if the results of the initial phone calls were an accurate gauge.

"I'll keep that in mind."

His attention abruptly focused across the room. "Hey, what's all this? Christmas decorations?"

Before she could stop him, he covered the distance to the holiday-designed boxes, crouched down, and popped the lid off one. "Oh, wow. I remember this."

He carefully lifted out a rustic-looking wooden crèche, a good eighteen inches tall and a maybe two feet wide. "This sat on the console table over there, didn't it? And baby Jesus never put in an appearance in the manger until Christmas morning."

"You have a good memory."

She moved to stand beside him as he continued

to rummage, reaching in for the Bubble-Wrapped wooden figurines and freeing them from their plastic-encased confines one at a time.

"Remember the year we nearly ransacked this place trying to find where your grandma hid baby Jesus so we could kidnap him?"

"You thought Grandma would pay the ransom in chocolate chip cookies."

"Brats, weren't we?" He lifted up a black-bearded wooden figurine, a wise man cloaked in a turquoise robe. "This guy, he was my favorite. Remember how we'd march them around, making them talk about the star and going in search of baby Jesus?"

"And got them into *Star Wars* battles along the way." She knelt down beside him and picked up one of the sheep. She hadn't seen this nativity set since she left for college. Since before they stopped coming to Hunter Ridge for Christmas when Grandma's health deteriorated.

Frowning, Garrett pawed through the plastic.

She placed the sheep down next to the other pieces. "What are you looking for?"

He dug around a bit more, then sat back on his heels, a solemn look on his face. "Sorry you lost your baby, Jodi."

Her breath caught, a wave of cold flooding her body as her gaze flew to his. How did he—

"Hey, Jode, don't look so distraught." He patted her arm in consolation. "I'm sure baby Jesus will turn up by Christmas Day. He always did, didn't He?"

Chapter Five

"Hey, isn't that Jodi over there, coming out of Dix's Woodland Warehouse?"

At his friend Drew Everton's words, Garrett's attention jerked from the menu at Camilla's Café in nearby Canyon Springs, and he turned to stare out the snowflake-decorated window by their table. It was Jodi all right, bundled against the cold in what looked to be a new turquoise jacket. New knee-high boots, too, which complemented her shapely, jeans-clad legs. As always, that long red-gold hair was an identity giveaway.

"Yeah. That's her." He once again studied the menu in his hands, unwilling to analyze why his heart rate had picked up a notch.

Inching his wheelchair forward, Drew reached across the table to flatten Garrett's menu on the table with the palm of his hand.

Startled, Garrett looked into the amused expression of his longtime friend. "What?"

"You are such a loser."

"What do you mean?" He pried the menu out from under Drew's fingers.

"Jodi. She's back in town after all these years, and you're determined to play it cool."

"There's nothing to play it cool about. Jodi and I are friends. Nothing more."

"Only because you're too dense to make it something more. The last time she came back to town when we were seniors in high school, she was a tomboy caterpillar that crawled out of its chrysalis as a beautiful butterfly. And don't tell me you didn't notice or I'll call you out as a liar, Pastor."

"Her transformation would have been a little hard not to notice," he conceded. "But Jodi and I've been pals since early grade school. I don't think either of us has ever seriously considered the other to be a romantic interest."

That wasn't a lie—as long as *seriously* was thrown in there.

Drew shook his head as he picked up his own menu. "You were so tied up in knots back then when the other guys caught a glimpse of her at the Christmas Eve service, it was laughable."

He had been. Richard was practically drooling and egging the rest of them on to see who could steal a kiss first. He'd had to do some quick thinking to remind them that Jodi was still Jodi—and likely still capable of defending herself. Not that she'd tried to defend herself from him earlier that night, although she probably wished she had.

"I was caught off guard, that's all. Don't tell me you weren't."

Drew snickered. "And you're still caught off guard? Is that the excuse you're going to give for letting her walk out of your life again?"

"I told you, Jodi and I—"

"Hey—" Drew nodded toward the window. "There she is again. Go catch her. Invite her to join us for lunch."

"I don't think—" He didn't relish the idea of her and Drew becoming reacquainted. Sooner or later the topic of how he'd sustained his life-altering injury would come up, and she'd realize her long-ago concerns about her childhood pal's bent toward high jinks and risk taking had sucked Drew into its whirlpool.

"Go get her, Garrett. You know I can't dash across the street." Drew leaned forward. "And if you won't do it for yourself, do it for me. Since you aren't interested in her, maybe I am."

Didn't Drew have enough gals fawning over him already? Enough that, as Garrett knew, it put one sweet little gal who had a serious interest in him at a disadvantage.

Irritated and not meeting his friend's gaze, he got up and stepped outside—coatless—then jogged across the street to the tune of a jolly holiday song played from strategically placed overhead speakers. He met up with Jodi as she reached Rio's truck.

"Garrett, what are you doing here? And where's your coat? It's freezing."

He wouldn't argue with that, but her smile, as always, warmed him.

"I'm having lunch with Drew. We get together every few weeks for guy talk. How about you? Shopping?"

"I am. How do you like the boots?" Gripping a colorful shopping bag in one hand and her purse in the other, she lifted her foot and turned her ankle this way and that to show them off. "Those old ones at the cabin weren't quite my style."

"Nice."

"Shopping is a sideline, though." The wind ruffled her hair, the red-gold glinting in the sunshine. "I actually came over to meet with my Canyon Springs Christian Church counterparts on the Christmas project—Kara Kenton and Meg Diaz, along with the pastor, who is Kara's brother-in-law. I felt a little nervous the whole time, though—Kara looks like her own expected baby could put in an appearance any minute now."

"Maybe she'll have a Christmas delivery." He

rubbed his chilled hands together. "How's the project doing here?"

"Great. I have to admit I'm jealous. I made a few more calls yesterday after you and Dolly left, and several said they'd already donated baby stuff to the project not that long ago. I was under the impression it was significantly more than that package of diapers we found in the storeroom."

"Melody may have gotten an emergency call and felt it best not to hold back, thinking she could easily make it up with additional donations." His office assistant had a big heart and didn't like to see anyone in need. "Have you talked to her?"

"I left a message, but no, not yet."

"Well, don't worry too much about it. You're barely getting started." He glanced back toward the café where he knew Drew would be watching his every move. "Hey, I don't know what your plans are for the rest of your day, but Drew and I were wondering if you'd be our lunchtime guest. We'd just sat down when we spied you across the street."

At least his old buddy wouldn't talk about his injuries in front of Garrett. He could be counted on to dodge questions if Jodi asked him outright. Oddly, he and Drew seldom talked about the day they'd been goofing off along the river that had carved out the depths of the Grand Canyon. About how Garrett should have known better. Been more responsible. After all, he was the experienced river guide—one who'd badgered his buddy into a rafting trip.

"I still have a lot to do this afternoon, but that would be wonderful." Her smile widened as she stowed her bag in the truck. "I'd been hoping to touch base with Drew while I'm here."

She had? *Guess I'll play chaperone then. My good deed for the day.* But the thought didn't please him.

Inside the cheerfully decorated restaurant and out of the cold, he helped her off with her coat. She left her woolen scarf draped around her neck as he pulled out a chair for her between him and Drew.

"So what have you been doing with yourself since high school, Drew?" She smiled up at a waitress who handed her a menu.

"College first, then missions work around the globe—predominantly in the Middle East, a region I've long had a heart for. Emergency relief. Digging wells."

"Wow."

"Of course, that was before this." He rapped his knuckles on the arm of his wheelchair, and Garrett winced. "Now I'm active in missions support for quite a few ministries."

Jodi tilted her head in interest. "What's that involve?"

"Prayer, first off." Drew set aside his menu to give her his full attention. "Then constant communication. Developing newsletters targeted to supporters, arranging travel, setting up sabbatical schedules and overseeing home-front things like financial assistance for missionary kids who are nearing college age."

"That would certainly keep you busy."

Drew grinned, obviously lapping up her attention. "Never a dull moment, that's for sure."

Fortunately, the waitress returned at that moment to take their orders, then the conversation drifted to how Canyon Springs, about thirty minutes from Hunter Ridge, had grown in recent years. A new equestrian center was drawing visitors to special events, the Lazy D Campground and RV Park had plans for expansion, and several new shops were popping up on Main Street. The annual regional charity fund-raising dinner was to take place here in town on Friday night. Garrett's cousin Grady and Grady's fiancée, Sunshine, would be representing the Hunter's Hideaway clan this year.

As they ate lunch, the topic evolved into the good old days of growing up in their own small town. There was a great deal of laughter and poking fun as they reminisced, and Garrett felt himself relaxing despite Drew's challenge that

if Garrett wasn't interested in Jodi, he himself
might be.

His buddy was ribbing him, right?

"So, Jodi," Drew ventured as he poised to finish off his roast beef sandwich, "you said you're
here to work on the cabin? That may be the line
you're feeding folks, but I have a sneaking sus-
picion there's more to it than that."

Apparently Garrett wasn't the only one wondering where Drew was going with this, because
Jodi raised a startled gaze to his friend.

Her throat suddenly dry, Jodi reached for her
water glass.

"You know," Drew prodded, with a chuckle,
"that you might actually have missed me and the
good pastor here? That you couldn't wait to get
back and renew our acquaintance?"

What was it with her? She had to stop reading things into simple conversation. She'd almost
passed out yesterday when Garrett made that remark about her losing a baby. *Baby Jesus*, for cry-
ing out loud. She'd taken his words out of context.
And being around the pregnant Kara Kenton that
morning had filled her with regrets. Why was it
all coming to the surface again? Because Garrett
was a pastor now—official guardian of all things
moral and good?

But jumping to the conclusion that Drew had

zeroed in on her inner turmoil? She was losing it big-time. Nevertheless, she managed a laugh. "You caught me, Drew. I haven't had anyone around in years to give me anywhere as near a hard time as the two of you do."

She glanced at Garrett, who seemed to be watching her closely. Had he sensed she hadn't come clean in her glib response to his friend? Looking up at the clock on the wall, she placed her napkin to the side of her plate. "I'm sorry to dash off, but I have a busy afternoon ahead. Sorting to do and more phone calls to make."

Drew gave her a curious look. "Phone calls?"

"I'm soliciting donations for the church Christmas project."

"*Our* church Christmas project?"

She nodded, and Drew slowly turned to stare at Garrett. "I can see what you're getting out of this, buddy. But what's in it for her?"

"He's helping clean the cabin," Jodi said, for some reason compelled to jump to Garrett's defense.

Drew hiked a brow, his tone dry. "*He's* cleaning the cabin?"

"He's making arrangements for someone to," she clarified.

"Figures."

Garrett gave his friend an annoyed look. "I intend to help—delivering firewood and replacing smoke alarms and cleaning out the shed. But the reason she's organizing the project is that no one else at the church would volunteer to do it at this late date, and I have my hands full with other responsibilities."

Drew smirked, then turned again to Jodi. "You didn't have anything better to do with your time?"

"Call me sentimental. I'm told that when my grandma spent the holidays in town, she liked to be involved in this particular ministry."

Drew nailed Garrett with a frown. "You made that up, didn't you? To get Jodi to help."

She laughed. "No, he didn't. Grandma's friends assure me she enjoyed being a part of it. I want to honor her memory by filling in."

Maybe helping would somehow make amends to Grandma, too, for her own failings and unwed state of pregnancy. And win brownie points with Garrett? Good luck with that one.

"That's generous of you." Drew cut another look at Garrett. "But don't go letting this guy take advantage of the goodness of your heart. He may be a preacher now, and with the way God's been blessing the socks off his ministry here, we'll be stuck with him for a good long while. But that's not yet made him eligible for sainthood."

"Far from it," Garrett mumbled the admission.

"I promise I'll keep him in his place, Drew." Amused at Garrett's apparent discomfiture and

Drew's obvious glee, she stood and Garrett instantly rose to help her into her coat. "I guess I'll see you two around."

"Guaranteed." Drew's comment was underlined with a smile, but she caught Garrett's unexpected frown.

Garrett lowered his voice as he walked her to the door. "Let's see about getting together tomorrow afternoon. Inventorying what's been donated so far."

Did he not feel that constant undercurrent running between them? That vibe of tension? No, of course he didn't. It was her own one-sided take on things. A pitiful hope that wouldn't die a merciful death. "I'll have to see what my schedule looks like."

Outside, the sun had once again disappeared behind gray-bottomed clouds. She'd enjoyed lunch with the comrades of her youth, but she felt like such a phony.

Drew was devoting his life to aiding ministries worldwide. Garrett was the pastor of a growing church, although she still had a hard time getting her head around *that* one. Both were men living life with faith-filled purpose. They weren't pretending to have it all together. Weren't hiding secrets that stained their soul. Nor were they masking doubts as to God's love or a bone-deep certainty that He was greatly disappointed in them.

She'd just climbed inside her loaner truck and shut the door when her cell phone chimed a tune.

"You've got to jump on this, Jodi." Her friend and former coworker Brooke Calvetti's voice vibrated with excitement. "I heard today that they're posting two more openings here for project managers. Full-time positions with beaucoup benefits. All virtual. Working from home like I am from wherever you want to plunk down your bod."

Like Jodi, Brooke had worked at SmithSmith since college graduation. In fact, they'd first become acquainted at the company's new-employee orientation. But when a few months ago rumblings started about offshoring their positions, Brooke hadn't hesitated. She'd given notice and was now settling into life at a new company. Unfortunately, her abrupt departure had put more pressure on Jodi to accept a position to train and supervise the new overseas workers.

"It sounds as if you're liking the new job."

"Liking it? Are you kidding me? I love it. You've got to get your application in. Now. With the way the economy's been, people are going to pounce on this."

But where would she go to set up a home base? While she loved Philadelphia, it was a long way from family. She'd had sporadic experience working from home in Philly after starting at Smith-Smith—the timing being such that she could conveniently keep her morning sickness under the radar. So she was familiar with the pros and cons of it. Both the freedom and the isolation.

It would be nice not to travel great distances at peak holiday seasons—she hadn't made it home for Thanksgiving in years. Missed some Christmases, too, when planes were grounded in a snowstorm. But even though working from home in the future would mean she might not have to deal with a commute in bumper-to-bumper traffic across the sprawling metropolis of Arizona's Valley of the Sun, the thought of baking-hot summers in Phoenix didn't appeal. She hated being trapped inside air-conditioned buildings, too.

Denver? San Diego, maybe?

"Have you looked at their website?" Brooke persisted. "This company is everything it claims and then more. You owe it to yourself to check it out."

"I'll take a look tonight. I promise." And she would. Sticking her head in the sand hoping that something would change at SmithSmith so she wouldn't have to make a decision would be foolish. As her mother always said, choosing not to make a decision was a decision in and of itself.

"Just think, Jodi, you can move wherever you

want to and only have to fly to the corporate office maybe quarterly at most."

That sounded good. Maybe too good to be true. After all, the grass always looked greener on the other side, and Brooke had barely climbed over the fence.

Jodi gazed down Canyon Springs' main street, at the holiday decorations and the bustle of activity. Cities offered so much, but there was something appealing about a small town. At that moment, she spied Garrett and Drew coming out of Camilla's Café and regret tugged at her heart.

If only Garrett hadn't always seen her as his little sister.

If only she hadn't messed her life up when she'd moved to Philadelphia.

If only…she hadn't come back to Hunter Ridge.

Chapter Six

Still no answer. Pausing in the buffeting wind outside the Hunter Ridge Artists' Cooperative midmorning Wednesday, Garrett pocketed his cell phone. Every time he tried to touch base with his office assistant to get further direction on the Christmas project, Melody's number went to messaging. He sure hoped it wasn't because her father had taken a turn for the worse.

Maybe it was just as well, though, that he not be sticking his nose into something he'd relinquished to Jodi's oversight. She might not appreciate his interference. But yesterday she sounded stymied by the lack of progress, and while she told Drew she volunteered to honor her grandmother, she'd graciously refrained from admitting to his buddy that she'd been pressured by *him*.

Pulling open the wreath-decorated door to the Artists' Co-op, a bell chimed as he stepped inside. He was immediately greeted with a friendly wave by Sunshine Carston, his cousin Grady's fiancée, who managed the place and who, after the first of the year, would take a seat on the town council.

"How may I help you, Pastor McCrae?" Her brown eyes sparkled as she brushed back a strand of shoulder-length jet-black hair. "Christmas shopping?"

"Sort of." He drew in the faint scent of oil paints and leather mingling with a holiday-ish pinch of cinnamon. "Actually, I'm trying to find a replacement piece for a nativity set. A baby Jesus, to be exact."

Just as a backup. Jodi's grandma's figurine would probably be found before Christmas Day. But although he'd teased her about how baby Jesus had always turned up in the past, for a flashing moment Jodi had appeared genuinely distressed when he told her he couldn't find the baby in the box with the other pieces.

"Is it broken? Maybe one of our artists can fix it for you."

"Missing."

"AWOL Jesus. Not good." Sunshine motioned him over to a display glass in the middle of the store. "Something like this?"

He leaned in to study several sets of figurines of the holy family. While striking, unfortunately all held a Southwestern-flavored simplicity rendered in terra-cotta and turquoise colors. Very unlike the traditional set belonging to Jodi's grandmother. The pieces here, too, were significantly smaller than those at the cabin. Mrs. Thorpe's Joseph was a good nine or ten inches tall. And carved from wood.

"Beautiful work, but not quite what I'm looking for."

Sunshine grimaced. "I hate to lose local business, but you might try an internet search."

"Last resort, but thanks for the suggestion."

He'd just stepped back outside when coming toward him with a determined step was Jodi, her coat hood pulled up against the cold. Their eyes met, and his spirits inexplicably lifted as she came to a halt next to him.

"What brings you out on this blustery day, Jodi?"

She let out a sigh. "I searched all over the cabin last night and still haven't found Grandma's baby Jesus. I can't have my nieces and nephew waking up to an empty manger. My sisters would never forgive me for that. Any ideas on where I might be able to find a replacement?"

He tipped his head toward the Artists' Co-op, but was reluctant to admit he was engaged in a similar pursuit. "You won't find what you're looking for in there."

"I never realized how unique Grandma's set is—and how large."

"Who will take possession of it once the cabin is sold?"

"We wouldn't want to split up the figurines. I guess…" A wrinkle furrowed her brow. "I guess if Mom and Dad don't want it at their place, it would go to Ronda or Star. You know, because they have children who will eventually inherit that piece of our grandparents' legacy."

She didn't look happy about that realization, though, and he wished he hadn't asked. Of the three girls, Jodi always seemed the most fascinated with the elaborate crèche scene even at an early age.

"I don't really have a place in my apartment to put something that big," she admitted. "And I certainly won't if I'm forced to accept an offer to transfer within the company I work for."

"You may be relocating?"

"I've been asked to take an overseas commitment. My company is offshoring a number of divisions, and as a primary project manager for one of those segments, I'm expected to be on-site as well. *India*."

"That's a big change."

"One I'm not real excited about. I've made trips there on business before and think it's a beautiful and diverse country. But living outside the US for any length of time isn't for me." She tucked a stray strand of red-gold hair back under her hood. "I'm one of the fortunate few who are being given an option to remain with the company. A lot of people are being laid off. But I'm beginning to rethink my options."

"I hope it works out."

A sudden gust of wind blew back Jodi's hood and, without thinking, he reached out both hands and pulled it up. Snugged it around her pretty face.

Her startled gaze met his, and lost in the beauty of her eyes, he slowly and self-consciously withdrew his hands. Stepped back. "Nippy out here."

"It is."

Conscious that anyone seeing them might wonder what they were doing standing outside staring at each other, he cleared his throat. "Things coming along on the cabin?"

"Slowly. Grandma's most personal things, of course, were removed years ago. But it's still slow going. Lots of memories to wade through."

"I imagine that's true. Good memories, fortunately."

"I'm blessed in that respect. A lot of families don't have that kind of foundation."

"Your grandma would be very proud of who you've become, Jodi."

She looked to him doubtfully as she braced

herself against another blast of wind. "Why do you say that?"

"You're a fine young woman. Mature. Talented. You've worked hard to get where you are professionally, yet family—and God—still play a part in your life and influence your values and decisions."

She ducked her head slightly. Embarrassed at the praise? To avoid the wind? Or maybe he was coming across as too pastor-like, not her familiar childhood chum who'd have been more likely to tease her to tears than heap praises on her.

"I try," she admitted, thrusting her gloved hands into her jacket pockets.

"Will I be seeing you this afternoon?"

She gave him a blank look.

"Remember? Yesterday at lunch? I said I'd help you inventory the donations."

"Oh, right. But I know you're swamped with pastor stuff right now. That's the whole reason you asked me to help out, remember?"

He cracked a smile. "Maybe I'll be ready for a break."

But how wise was it to find excuses to spend time with Jodi? Was he secretly hoping for a glimmer of evidence that her sisterly feelings for him had shifted? But with him preparing to leave town shortly, what could possibly come of it? Too much water under the bridge.

She offered a smile of her own, albeit a slightly tight one. "Whatever works for you."

Maybe the way things ended when they were teenagers still made her uncomfortable. He wasn't enamored with the thought of apologizing at this point, though. That reminder of how he'd over-stepped his bounds might make her even more ill at ease.

And if there was anything he didn't want right now, it was to make Jodi uncomfortable around him, brotherly feelings or not.

Grandma would be proud of her? Not likely.

Jodi carried a stack of baby blankets to one of the tables in the church's fellowship hall and set them down among the other accumulating dona-tions. Grandma wouldn't have turned her back on her, but she'd have been deeply disappointed in her oldest granddaughter. Saddened and hurt that she'd so thoughtlessly distanced herself from her family values and the commitment she'd pledged to God in her early teens.

No, Garrett, Grandma would not be proud.

And what would Grandma now think of the fact that even after the humiliation Garrett had dealt her when she was sixteen, she couldn't get him out of her head a dozen years later? She felt skittish around him. Acted weird. He'd merely done something nice this morning in pulling her windblown hood back up, yet she'd frozen like a deer in the headlights. He'd probably helped her get her hood back on dozens of times when they were growing up. Of course, back then he'd have pulled it down over her face.

But it was ridiculous to be crushing on him at her age. And even if he did show interest, there was no way once he learned of her past, discovered the status of her faltering faith, that he'd remain interested. Besides, she still hadn't figured out where Sofia Ramos fit into the picture.

Jodi stepped back to survey the tables and clear her head. Where should she start? When she had arrived at the church after lunch, Dolly said Pastor McCrae was out of the office, so hopefully she could get this stuff sorted and inventoried before he put in an appearance.

"You're here already." Garrett strolled into the fellowship hall as he peeled out of a leather jacket, then draped it over the back of a folding chair next to her. He smelled enticingly of the fresh, cold outdoors.

Ah, well. Best-laid plans. "I wanted to get this done as quickly as possible so when I start making calls again, I can provide better suggestions for what's really needed."

He put his hands on his hips, his brows tenting. "When I recruited you, I genuinely thought it would be a slam dunk. Needing only to be tied up with a pretty bow."

"Well, we'll get to the pretty bow stuff eventually, but right now it looks like I have my work cut out for me." At his glum look, she hurried on. "I've worked on lots of other projects and it always seems you reach a plateau point. You know, where the goal looks to be entirely out of reach. Not going to happen. Then suddenly it all comes together."

With a little over a week before delivery time, though, they'd better start moving off the plateau soon.

"We do have a budget of sorts to supplement. There are members of the community—like Sawyer Banks, owner of the Echo Ridge Outpost—who don't know exactly what to buy and who've made cash contributions. Once we get this inventoried, we can do some shopping."

We? He intended to help inventory the donations and go shopping with her, too?

She'd brought her laptop and pointed to it. It was opened to a document with a boldly typed header: Christmas Project. The cursor blinked in silent anticipation. "Do you want to announce the items we've received as I type a list? Or vice versa?"

"Vice versa, I think." He pulled up a folding

chair. "I'm not sure I'd know what half of these things even are."

And *she* would? Except when she'd all but been drafted into pitching in with her nieces and nephew when they were infants, she'd avoided tiny kids at all costs. Being around them only brought regret and heartache.

"Okay, then, you type. And we'll make an educated guess on the things we're not sure about."

He settled himself in front of the laptop, fingers poised over the keys, then shot her a heart-stopping grin. "Ready when you are."

As she went from table to table, naming off the items, bits and pieces of conversation of a more personal nature interspersed. He asked for an update on her folks—were they still teaching at the university? Taking mission trips during the summer and holidays? Yes to both.

He asked about her sisters—where they and their husbands lived and worked. How old their children were. In turn, she inquired about his family and received a rundown on the members of the extended Hunter's Hideaway clan, as well as a catch-up on his younger brother Marc and sister Jenna, now a single mother who'd only recently returned to town.

The conversation drifted comfortably along, a nostalgic reminder of times the two of them would shoot baskets or hang out on the front porch playing games or make improvements to their woodland fort. Back then they'd talk for hours on end about anything that popped into their heads. The conversation today likewise meandered.

Then, out of the blue, Garrett asked if she was seeing anyone, and the easy banter came to a halt. Was he hoping to set her up with one of his buddies? Drew, maybe? She held no delusions that he was asking on his own behalf.

She picked up one of the packages of baby bibs and inspected it, although it was an item she'd already called off to him. "Not at the moment."

She cringed inwardly, realizing that response would give the impression she was available for whomever he had in mind.

"I haven't dated for some time." Although that was an admission she'd have preferred not to make, she plunged on. "But that's by choice. I'd previously been seeing a man—a missionary to Mexico—through my church in Philly."

It was a church that she should have gotten involved with when she'd first moved there. If she'd surrounded herself with other believers from the very beginning, maybe none of the things that had shaken her world down to its foundations would have happened. But she'd already been drifting away during college, and afterward she'd been so busy acclimating to city life and her new job—and then she'd met Kel O'Connor...

"Anton and I corresponded and got together whenever he was back in the States. His family lived in Philadelphia, too."

"That didn't work out?"

Because of her. She'd met Anton a year after Kel and the baby, when she'd in desperation begun going to church again. And although he was a wonderful guy in so many ways, she'd dragged her feet when he expressed an interest. The following year when he was in Philly, she'd been forced to turn him away when he'd wanted to marry her.

How could she have married him without telling him the truth about herself? About the baby? About her still-flatlined faith even though she warmed a pew each week?

"No, it didn't work out. It was for the best for both of us. But then...then he died last month." Two years after she'd sent him away, but his sister had provided the details. "There was a medical emergency in the remote village his team was working in and he volunteered to hitchhike out to bring help. But those who picked him up robbed, beat and murdered him. All for the few pesos in his pocket."

His empty, discarded wallet, she'd been told, held a photo of the two of them.

"Oh, man, Jodi." Garrett rose and came to her side to place a comforting hand on her arm. "I'm sorry."

She took a ragged breath, turning the package of baby bibs mindlessly in her hands. "Here was a man who served God so faithfully, who was endeavoring to be God's hands and feet in a place most wouldn't choose to set foot in. I've asked so many times—where was God that day?"

"I know how hard things like this are to understand." A distinct sadness filled his eyes. Compassion for her, or a wound of his own? "This isn't how God intended His creation to be. Granting mankind free will to love Him—or not—has come at a high cost. But it doesn't mean He's abandoned us."

"But why lose one of the good guys? It seems so senseless."

"It does. But we can't allow circumstances to dictate to us what *appears* to be a truth about God. We *can*, though, choose to believe what God tells us is the truth about circumstances. That He will never leave us or forsake us. That Christ *is* coming back. That's a fact. And one day He'll make everything right again."

"I wish I had your faith."

He gave her arm a reassuring squeeze. "It only takes belief the size of a mustard seed to please God, Jodi. Belief that He exists and that He's a rewarder of those who seek Him. I think your… friend…had that kind of faith."

"He did. And more. Anton was happy doing what he believed God wanted him to do." But if she'd agreed to marry him, might he have chosen a less dangerous mission in which to serve? Might he still be alive today if she'd been courageous enough to risk telling him about her shadowed past? "At least it's comforting to know he died doing what he wanted to do. And lived his life with passion and purpose."

"But it doesn't take the pain away, does it? Or the questions."

She shook her head. "No."

"I'm sorry for your loss, Jode. Even though you said things hadn't worked out between the two of you, I know this hurts."

"It does. In fact, it's one of the main reasons I came to Hunter Ridge. To have time to work through things. The job. Anton. Not just to fix up the cabin to sell."

"Then I saddled you with this." He motioned to the tables. "I'd be happy to check around again for another volunteer."

"Please don't. I think it's actually helped to have something else to think about occasionally."

He looked at her doubtfully. "You're sure?"

She nodded. Then tossed the package of baby bibs to the table. "Let's finish things up here so I can get back to the cabin and start making more phone calls."

"Or…" A smile tugged at the corners of Garrett's mouth. "We *could* go shopping."

Chapter Seven

Heading out of town to the discount warehouse in Canyon Springs, it felt a little odd having Jodi in the passenger seat beside him and Dolly in the back acting as guardian of his reputation. Although Jodi offered her the front seat, Dolly waved a paperback at them and insisted she didn't want to stop reading. If she sat in the front, she'd feel obligated to join the conversation, and she *had* to find out "whodunit."

That was Dolly for you. Come rain or shine— or a snowy day like today—this past year she'd been ungrudgingly willing to serve as chaperone as needed, even if it wasn't personally convenient. But, while appreciated, the need for one had become increasingly stifling—and doubly so since Jodi's return. More like he had a warden.

At least the roads were good today, although the roadside and forest floor were layered in white. Snowflakes danced in the air as another squall passed through. Interspersed with brief bouts of blue sky and sunshine that warmed the blacktopped surface, days like this made winter a bit easier to bear.

He glanced in the rearview mirror at Dolly engrossed in her book, then at Jodi who was quietly gazing out the side window at the passing snowy world.

He didn't know why he suggested they go shopping for the Christmas project this afternoon. Shopping would be better done next week when they had a true handle on what was still needed. But while he was only somewhat concerned that they wouldn't meet their collection goal for the project, Jodi seemed especially troubled by her lack of progress. He didn't like the thought, either, of her retreating to an empty cabin to make phone calls while the memories he'd stirred up about the loss of a former love were fresh in her mind.

When telling him about her job, how it was being relocated overseas, she'd stated that she didn't want to live outside the country. Had that played a role in keeping the two apart?

"Oh, look! An elk." Jodi's face brightened as she pointed out the window, and sure enough, through the tall-trunked pines he glimpsed a male elk with an impressive set of antlers moving among the trees. "There were two deer behind the cabin this morning. I hope they come back while my sisters' kids are here."

"I never tire of seeing them myself," Dolly chimed in before disappearing once again into her mystery.

Garrett and Jodi exchanged a smile, and a sense of contentment burrowed into his soul as they continued to talk about wildlife, the beauty of the Arizona mountains, the blessings they'd shared growing up—if only part-time for Jodi—in Hunter Ridge. Funny, but for a long time he hadn't seen the town—or his return to it—as much of a blessing. But somehow that perspective seemed easier to embrace as the months in his new position passed by. As he chatted with Jodi about it, relived memories, a deep sense of thankfulness took hold.

She peeped over at the SUV's speedometer and grinned. "I see you're still lead-footed, Pastor."

He eased off the gas pedal, enjoying the sound of her laughter. "Remember when I first got my license when I turned sixteen and took you for a drive?"

"I do. You already had a reputation for drag racing, and I think Grandma was down on her knees in prayer the whole time we were gone."

He chuckled. Having Jodi around these past few days had been good for him. Like now, they often fell into old patterns of talking about anything that they felt like talking about. Teasing each other. Challenging each other. It was an easiness he hadn't often felt except when around family members once he'd walked through the formal gates of pastoring a church. With Jodi, though, he could let down his guard and be himself, something he had to be cautious about with church and community members—especially single women.

He tried to live a transparent life, not to put on a fake pastor-y persona, but with Jodi's return, he could now see how much he'd come to subconsciously weigh each word, each action. Of course, there were those who clearly thought he could work a little harder at being "pastor-like," unable to recognize how much he'd already reined in his naturally exuberant personality.

When they arrived at the discount warehouse, Dolly pried herself away from her book to join them, but quickly disappeared into the cavernous space with her own oversize shopping cart.

As he and Jodi strolled down the wide aisles with merchandise of every assortment towering high above their heads, an unfamiliar sense of domesticity thrummed through him. People passing by, seeing them each at the helm of a cart and hearing their discussion as they filled the baskets, might easily take them for a couple. A married couple.

He shook the thought from his head as Jodi held up a package of—what did she call them? Onesies? Infant wear, they looked to be.

"Some of these?"

He nodded. "What do you think? Ten packages? Twelve?"

"Twelve. We didn't have many of these among the donations." She counted them out and put them in her cart, then checked them off their list.

And so they proceeded among the display tables and racks, filling her oversize cart with clothing items for newborns through toddlers. Then stops to load up on baby wipes, lotions and other assorted paraphernalia soon filled his.

It was fun—and kind of funny, actually, as neither had a clue as to what a baby might need if it hadn't been for Melody's checklist.

Laughing as they rounded a corner in search of Dolly, a firm voice halted them in their tracks.

"Well, *Pastor.* You two look to be having a high old time."

Randall Moppert, accompanied by his wife, Leona, swept a disapproving gaze from Garrett to Jodi and back again.

"We are indeed, Randall. Almost as much fun as the night I TP'd your house." Now where'd that smart-aleck response come from?

Curly-haired Leona giggled, then abruptly halted when her husband, his graying mustache twitching, sent her a squelching glance. But her eyes still smiled. The woman had to be a saint to have lived with Randall all these years.

"Serving as a minister of God requires a certain level of decorum, Mr. McCrae. You'd do well to remember that." Randall's beady eyes narrowed as he motioned dismissively to their laden carts. "And what's all this anyway?"

"The church's Christmas project," Jodi inserted, not caring for the man's tone of voice as he reprimanded Garrett. She'd encountered him at church a number of times, usually when he was complaining about something. "Gifts for unwed mothers."

His smirk and the arrogant raising of his thick brows did nothing to endear him to her. "I've never approved of that annual effort myself—rewarding promiscuous young women for getting themselves in a family way."

His words pierced, and Jodi lifted her chin slightly to meet his condemning gaze. "They didn't get that way all by themselves."

He snorted. "Nevertheless—"

"We're supporting them, Randall, not rewarding them," Garrett said evenly. "They've chosen to honor the sanctity of life and not have an abortion. And we reach out to them because that's what Jesus would have done."

"I think it's a nice thing to do," the man's wife said softly, ignoring her husband's shriveling glare.

The man leveled a look at Garrett and Jodi. "Which doesn't, however, explain why the two of you are gallivanting off by yourselves in a neighboring town. A single pastor and a single woman."

"They aren't gallivanting off by themselves, Randy." Coming into view as she pushed a filled cart around the corner, Dolly smiled benignly at the old curmudgeon. "They brought me with them so I could shop while they attend to church business."

While Garrett's insistence on not being alone with her had irked Jodi, now she could see the wisdom of it.

Looking somewhat taken aback—his hopes obviously thwarted from laying a misdeed on the doorstep of his pastor—the man tightened his grip on his shopping cart. "I guess we have *something* to be grateful for, then."

Dolly nodded. "We can always find something to be thankful for when we take the time to look for it."

Apparently not quite sure how to take her comment, he glanced at his wife. "Let's get on with this shopping. It's already taken too much of our afternoon."

When the couple departed, Jodi exchanged a glance with Garrett and Dolly, but none of them said any of the words they were no doubt thinking. How miserable that man must be, scrutinizing every innocent nook and cranny around him for evidence of questionable behavior. And his poor wife...

It was only when they were back in Hunter Ridge unloading Garrett's SUV in the church parking lot, the sun now sinking behind the towering ponderosas, that she reopened the topic.

"That Randall person had no business behaving so disrespectfully to you."

To her surprise, Garrett chuckled as he lifted two oversize bags from the back and handed them to her, not appearing the least bothered by the other man's disparaging remarks. "Randall Moppert is one of the church members who can't get beyond who I was as a teenager."

"From your comment to him, I take it you targeted his house for TP-ing?"

"By accident."

"Randy needs to let that go." Dolly took one of her own shopping bags from Garrett. "You've more than proven yourself to anyone who's allowed God to open their eyes and soften their hearts."

"Thanks, Dolly. But coming from a woman

who's all but adopted me, you're probably a little biased."

"I know a good thing when I see it. This church has a future as long as you're at the helm."

A flash of uncertainty flickered through Garrett's eyes, then he ducked his head slightly. Uncomfortable with the praise?

"I appreciate your appreciation, Dolly."

He hauled out three more bags, then motioned for the ladies to precede him to the door leading to the fellowship hall. While she and Dolly arranged the purchases in the storeroom, Garrett made several more trips out to his SUV.

"Looks like that about does it." He looked on approvingly as they accepted the last of the bags and added the contents to the growing stacks of items. The storeroom still wasn't full by any means, but they were getting there. "Did you want me to drop you off home now, Dolly?"

"No, I've called Al. He's going to pick me up, then we'll go out to eat since I wasn't home this afternoon to prepare anything. I'll wait inside until he gets here."

Garrett stuffed his gloves in his pockets. "Tell him I owe him. Big-time. A man who sacrifices his supper so his wife can babysit their pastor has a special place in Heaven."

"You know I'm more than happy to do it." She patted the bags sitting on the floor beside her. "I finished up my own holiday shopping and got a few things for Christmas dinner to boot."

"Well, there you go."

Jodi liked the way Garrett returned the older woman's smile with genuine affection.

Dolly tilted her head to look up at him. "You could walk Jodi to *her* car if you want to make yourself useful. It's almost dark."

"Oh, I'm fine," Jodi piped up. She'd need to brush off the snow that had accumulated while she'd been gone and didn't want Garrett to feel obligated to help with that when he had other things to see to. On the return trip, he'd mentioned conducting a marital counseling session early that evening for his cousin and his fiancée. He said that although Grady had originally balked at having his *single* relative instruct him, Sunshine had confidence in Garrett's ability to share the truths of God's word, and she'd proved quite persuasive in getting Grady signed up.

"I'm more than happy to do that." Garrett gave a nod to Dolly as he pulled on his gloves again.

Faint light lingered in the west, silhouetting the tree branches overhead as they stepped into the parking lot. The temperature had dropped considerably since leaving town earlier that afternoon, and Jodi tugged at her hood to snug it more closely around her face.

"Brr!"

"Brr is right," Garrett agreed as he turned up his own collar and gave her a lopsided grin. "You'd think this was the middle of December or something, wouldn't you?"

She laughed.

He shared a smile, then motioned to the truck as they approached it. "Rio has a snow brush or ice scraper, I take it?"

"She does, but you don't have to—"

"Pop on in there and get the heater going while I make short work of the snow."

Another gust of wind came out of the north, so it didn't take much to persuade her. She handed the combo brush and scraper to Garrett, then he slammed the door shut and she started up the truck. Flipped the defroster on full blast.

He worked quickly, brushing the snow off the hood and headlights, then made his way around to the taillights. It took a bit longer, though, even with the help of the defroster, to clean the windshield and back and side windows. To the rhythm of the scraper, she held her hands out to the heating vents and watched him in the dim light as he expertly sliced away the frozen snow that had almost melded itself to the glass.

She felt special, having someone like Garrett help her on a night like this. He was a good man. One any woman would be fortunate to have in her life. But dreams like that were for people who had time on their side. Time to get to know each other. To build bonds. For people who shared a mutual affection for each other—not a one-sided infatuation.

A wave of melancholy filled her heart as she continued to watch him, her mind drifting back in time. Back to that night when she thought, for a single, blissful moment, that maybe he felt something for her, too.

Abruptly, Garrett rapped on the driver's-side window, startling her from her reverie. He'd finished cleaning the windows and was motioning for her to roll hers down.

Cold from the open window swept into the cab. "Thanks, Garrett. Now you'd better get yourself inside before you turn into an ice cube."

"Actually, I was wondering…do you have plans for dinner?"

Her heart stilled. "Tonight, you mean?"

"Right now. I have to eat earlier than usual so I can get back to the church. Do you already have plans?"

"Not really. I thought maybe I'd warm a can of soup."

"Then join me. How's the Log Cabin Café sound? Or Rusty's Grill?"

"We can do that?"

A crease formed between his brows. "What do you mean?"

"I mean, *you* can do that? Go out to eat with me without Dolly riding shotgun?"

He laughed. "I can—*if* we walk. You know, if we're out in the open where people can keep an eye us. Are you up to that? It's only a few blocks, but it is bitter cold out here."

What would it hurt? It wasn't like it was a date or anything. They both had to eat, right? And if he didn't think showing up with her at a local dining establishment would sully his reputation, well, who was she to argue?

"Actually, my stomach's still on Eastern Time, so I'm starving."

"Then let's do it."

He handed her the scraper, then let her roll the window back up and turn off the truck before swinging the door open.

Once outside, he guided her to the sidewalk in front of the church, and they headed toward the main road through town. The steadily falling snow by turns danced, then whipped, around them depending on if they were walking in the open or alongside a building or sheltering stand of pines.

Except for the occasional gust of wind, it was a quiet evening, most people with any sense having decided to stay close to hearth and home. But this was kind of fun, too, walking beside Garrett as the snow crunched under their boots, a snow glow overhead and halos encircling the streetlights.

If only she could stop shaking.

Not from the cold, but from nervousness. Excitement. How silly. She'd enjoyed visiting with Garrett on the drive to and from Canyon Springs. They'd indulged in quiet moments and a fun-filled time of renewing their acquaintance as they refreshed memories. But she wasn't sixteen anymore. This wasn't a date. They were just two old friends grabbing a bite to eat. Nothing more.

Garrett jogged her elbow. "So does Rusty's sound good to you?"

"Perfect. I haven't had his barbecue since the last time we—"

Abruptly her mind flashed back a dozen years. After a morning's hike on snowy trails, they'd eaten there for lunch on Christmas Eve. Her. Garrett. Drew. She'd had no idea that not too many hours from then, Garrett would back her into a corner of Grandma's cabin mudroom and kiss her almost senseless.

Had *he* known? Planned it? Maybe even plotted it with Drew or any number of his other buddies looking for a good laugh at her expense? She glanced toward Garrett, but he was focused ahead as they neared the little restaurant.

"—not since you, Drew and I ate there," she

finished, the shaking anticipation now replaced by an unexpected heaviness in her chest.

"That's right. Christmas Eve." He smiled at her. "I'd forgotten we had lunch together that time you were in town."

That time she was in town...and the last time she'd let herself hope that Garrett might return her feelings.

Chapter Eight

Although he'd eaten at Rusty's Grill plenty of times in the last twelve years, it hadn't changed much since Jodi would have last been here. Its labyrinth of rustic, beamed-ceiling spaces made for a homey atmosphere, with flickering lanterns anchored to beadboard-paneled walls and woven plaid tablecloths accenting the stoneware dishes.

From where they sat at a small table near one of the fireplaces, Garrett leaned forward to get Jodi's attention.

"How's your barbecue?"

She glanced up from toying with her mason jar water glass. "Delicious."

But for a woman who'd claimed to be starving, she hadn't eaten a whole lot of her sandwich or sweet potato fries. His were long gone. "Are you feeling better about the Christmas project now? I mean, after we did that shopping today?"

"Yes, thank you. Those added items take some of the pressure off."

"I don't want you to feel pressured, Jodi." Without thinking, he slid his hand across the table to cover hers.

She lifted startled eyes and drew her hand from his. "I didn't mean it like that. I just meant it's good to know we have our bases covered. Somewhat, anyway."

He pulled his hand back as well and quickly glanced around the room at the other diners. Had anyone seen him reach out to her? But there weren't many people this early in the evening, and no one seemed to be paying them any attention. "We still have over a week. It will all come together."

"And next year Melody will be back and you'll be off the hook." She offered a smile as she pushed her unfinished plate slightly away from her.

He nodded to it. "Are you going to eat the rest of that, or would you like a to-go box?"

She glanced down, looking almost surprised to see over half of one of the best pulled-pork barbecue sandwiches in the state still sitting in front of her.

"It's very good," she said quickly, as though she needed to reassure him. As if not eating it might have hurt his feelings. "Yes, a box would be great. Thanks."

"Sure you don't want dessert? This place makes a mean pumpkin cheesecake, remember?"

She laughed, and the tension in his shoulders eased. He still wasn't quite sure how the comfortable atmosphere that lingered after the trip to Canyon Springs had become stiff and stilted by the time they'd settled in at Rusty's. Maybe she'd started thinking about that Anton guy again?

She shook her head at him, intimating he was as dense as a rock. "How could I forget Rusty's signature holiday cheesecake? I ordered one and you and Drew pulled out forks and proceeded to devour most of it when I had to slip off to the ladies' room."

"Then I owe you one."

He reached for the dessert menu, but with another shake of her head, she clasped her hand to her stomach. "Thanks, but I'm going to pass this time. There are already too many sweet temptations this time of year."

And speaking of sweet temptations…it was time he let this one get on home so he wouldn't be late to Grady and Sunshine's counseling session. He'd looked forward to extending his time with Jodi after the shopping trip, inexplicably happy that she'd agreed to go to dinner with him. But maybe it had been a bit too much togetherness? When you've exhausted your repertoire of shared memories, maybe you discover that's all you had?

He placed his napkin on the table. "Ready to go?"

She nodded, but before either could rise, a firm hand clapped him on the back.

"Well, look who's here."

Garrett turned to see a grinning Travis Hunter, cousin Luke's son, looking down at him as if he'd been let in on a big secret.

How old was he now? Sixteen? Seventeen? A good-looking kid, the unruly layers of hair brushing his shoulders always bringing a smile to Garrett. The boy's ex-military father had thrown in the towel on haircuts to keep the peace, just as Garrett's dad had been forced to do.

Garrett nodded to his young cousin, who was with his longtime girlfriend. A petite brunette with a pixie haircut and an abundance of eyeliner, she was a sweet, down-home gal despite her trendy looks.

"I can't believe you're still hanging around with this dude, Scottie."

Her smile widened as Travis gazed down at her. *Young love.* Had he looked at Jodi like that twelve years ago? So transparent? So...*goofy*?

He quickly made introductions, making sure he emphasized *old friends* so Travis wouldn't get the wrong idea and go running back to the family with what he might think was a scoop. It was bad enough having the teenager stand there grinning at them, his gaze bouncing from Jodi to Garrett and back again.

Garrett caught Jodi's eye, and they both stood.

Travis frowned. "You're leaving?"

"I have an early-evening counseling session with your Uncle Grady and his bride-to-be."

Travis laughed. "Sunshine's a quick learner, but you might have to schedule some remedial classes for him."

"I'll keep that in mind."

Eager to escape Travis's too-observant eye, Garrett motioned to Jodi, who preceded him to the front of the restaurant. Fortunately, she'd stepped around a corner before Travis gave him an exaggerated wink and a thumbs-up. No doubt he'd have some explaining to do at the next family dinner.

He settled the bill, fending off Jodi's insistence they split it as a thanks for her help. In the lobby, he assisted Jodi with her coat, then held the door open as they stepped into the still-frigid night.

"Look, Garrett. Isn't that beautiful?"

His gaze followed the trajectory of hers upward, where the clouds had parted to reveal a dark window of sky. There, a single star glittered.

Without thinking, he leaned in to whisper in her ear. "Star light, star bright…"

Surprised, she turned to him, her eyes questioning.

He pulled abruptly back and pushed his hands

into his jacket pockets as they started down the street. "Don't you remember that? How we'd sit out at night, competing to see who'd spy the first star?"

Maybe he could get her reminiscing again. Back to a comfortable conversation such as they'd shared earlier.

She rolled her eyes. "Get your story straight, mister. That was the first *shooting* star."

"Oh, yeah. That's right."

They walked on in silence for some time, snow crunching under their boots. The wind had died down while they were in Rusty's, so it wasn't a half-bad walk back to the church.

He stopped and turned to her. "Do you remember...naw, you wouldn't."

He moved off again, and she had to hurry to keep up.

"What?" She punched him lightly in the arm. "What wouldn't I remember?"

"You know, that afternoon we charged our sisters a quarter each for a cup of lemonade from the pitcher we'd sneaked out of your grandma's refrigerator."

She laughed. "Of course I remember that, silly. When word got back to Grandma, the next day at lunch she charged us a quarter for a sandwich, a quarter for chips and a quarter for a glass of milk."

"Lesson learned the hard way, huh?"

"We learned a lot of our lessons the hard way," she agreed.

He sure knew he had.

They entered the parking lot all too soon, and at her truck he waited for her to click the key she fished out of her pocket. The headlights flashed, then he opened the door. "Your coach awaits, madam."

With an almost shy smile, she curtsied, then climbed into the vehicle. The wind, fortunately, had served its purpose, keeping the windshield clear of snowfall since his earlier scraping.

He stood at the door, looking in at her. She was beautiful in the faint overhead snow glow, her hair spilling loosely around her shoulders. "I had a good time today, Jodi."

She gave him an uncertain look, as though not sure if she could agree or not. "I...did, too."

"You know you'll be the talk of the breakfast table at Hunter's Hideaway tomorrow morning, don't you?"

"Travis, you mean?"

"Guaranteed." Realizing he'd leaned a bit too close, he took a step back. "Guess I'll be seeing you tomorrow."

"Tomorrow?"

"Or maybe the next day. I said I'd clean out that shed for you, right?"

"If you have time."

"I'll make time."

He slammed the door, then moved away as she started the truck. The headlights came on, and with a parting wave, she backed out of the parking place and headed home.

He stood there in the dark for a full minute, then strode toward the church. Yeah, he'd make time.

"Thank you, Mrs. Garver. I'll be by to pick them up this afternoon." Thursday already. A week from tomorrow they'd make the delivery, so every donation counted.

Jodi checked another name off the list, but her happy dance around the room was soon interrupted by a knock at the side door. She turned down the CD player and hurried through the mudroom, then opened the door to Dolly.

"Come in, come in. Good news! The manager of the discount store donated three car seats. Diamond Grocery has promised formula. And Garrett's Grandma Jo is pitching in *again* with a few infant carriers that she ordered online. They should be here tomorrow."

"You're making headway."

Not as much as she'd like, but it was a start.

She helped Dolly with her coat, hung it up, and then followed her into the kitchen.

"How'd you get here, anyway?" Jodi asked. Dolly didn't like driving on icy roads if she could help it.

"Garrett."

"He's here?" She hadn't heard a vehicle, but after that last phone call she'd cranked up the volume on the Christmas music. "Is he here to clean out the shed? He'd mentioned yesterday that he might be over to do that."

"He brought a ladder, so I think he intends to clean the gutters. Those things fill with pine needles faster than you can blink an eye. Al bought us those covered ones last year. Worth every dime."

Jodi cast an anxious glance toward the refrigerator. "I'm not sure I have anything here that will make him a decent lunch. The two of us can have yogurt and fresh fruit, but that's not very substantial for a man."

"He's not staying long. He has to get back to the church. But either he or Al will pick me up later."

A twinge of disappointment that Garrett couldn't stay long caught her by surprise. He'd told her last night that he'd had a good time yesterday. He hadn't elaborated, though, so it might not mean anything more than he enjoyed a chance to get out of town. Or got his kicks shopping for baby stuff.

She'd had a good time, too, until the past intruded on her thoughts as they neared Rusty's. That uncomfortable meal was her fault. But the reminder of the last one they'd shared there offered a precautionary prelude to the evening—*guard your heart, girl*.

"So where should we start, Dolly? Bedrooms?"

"Let's turn the mattresses and pull everything out of the closets to sort through. Then if there's time, we can clean the floors. In the meantime, let's throw in a few loads of bedding for your visitors. Wash up the curtains, too."

"I think the flannel sheets are in the hall closet. Grandma kept those as a special treat for us in the wintertime. There was nothing more wonderful than cuddling into their toasty warmth."

They'd barely gotten started when she heard the back door open, the sound of boots stomping on the floor mat and the voice of an approaching Garrett echoing down the hall.

"Jodi, do you have any—hey!" He stood in the doorway, sock-footed but still bundled against the cold. "Let me do that. Neither of you should be manhandling a mattress."

He shooed them out of the way, then maneuvered into the room to make short work of flipping the mattress.

Dolly clasped her hands and brought them to her heart. "Our hero."

A grinning Garrett posed in a classic body-builder stance.

"Show-off." Jodi playfully poked him in the stomach, and he pretended to double over. "We could use your talents in the room next door, too, Mr. Muscle."

Eyes still smiling, he straightened up. "Lead on."

After turning the mattress in the adjacent room, he joined her in the hallway. "Do you have any garbage bags? You know, the big kind for yard work."

"I think I can accommodate that request. This way."

In the mudroom she opened a lower cabinet door, pulled out a box and handed it to him. "Voilà!"

"Exactly what I was looking for."

"Dolly says you're cleaning the gutters?"

"Yeah, and I want to get a replacement section for one of the downspouts. It's fairly beat-up. Looks, too, as if a few shingles need to be replaced."

She made a face. "The cabin's falling apart."

He laughed. "No, it's not. This is just a standard part of home maintenance. It's all good."

"I'm glad you know what you're doing. I sure wouldn't. You're a pastor of many talents."

"Bible College 101. Ark maintenance."

She folded her arms and leaned her hip against the counter. "Sometime, I want to hear about that. You know, how it all came about."

He quirked a smile. "God called. I came."

"Surely there was more to it than that." If she didn't know better, she'd think he was being evasive. But why would a minister be evasive about what led him to his Lord?

"Thanks, again." He lifted up the lawn bag box in acknowledgment, then moved to the door where he pulled on his boots.

"Garrett?"

"Yeah?" He looked at her, an almost wariness in his eyes.

That had to be nothing more than her imagination. He had a lot to get done in a short amount of time and probably didn't want to pause for a long conversation.

She'd halted him in his tracks, delayed his departure, but did she really have anything worthwhile to say to him? Or was she being stupid again? Once more forgetting this was the guy who'd broken her heart. Who'd be disappointed in her if he ever discovered her secrets.

"We got more donations."

Did she also imagine the relief in his eyes?

"Awesome. I told you things would pick up, didn't I?"

"You did. But we still have a long way to go. I'm securing a few car seats this afternoon, but we don't have many of the other big-ticket items like high chairs. Or strollers. Or portable cribs."

She wished she didn't sound like such a Debbie Downer. He'd put her in charge so he wouldn't have to deal with the details. But he'd also told her if she didn't want to do this, he'd find another volunteer. Is that what she wanted him to do?

No. He was helping her get the cabin ready to sell, and she'd keep her part of the bargain.

She squared her shoulders. "I'll make more phone calls throughout the day today and will do my best to emphasize the need for some of those items."

"Sounds like a plan." He gave her a thumbs-up, then once more turned toward the door.

"Garrett?"

He paused again, and it was all she could do not to flat-out ask him what had drawn him away from the river. From the passion that had possessed him since he was a teenager. Had there been a woman involved?

"What's up?"

"I—just want to thank you again for all you're doing to help me with the cabin."

"You're welcome."

He winked. And was out the door.

Chapter Nine

"I'd forgotten your grandparents had so much kid stuff." Garrett, standing inside the small metal shed in back of the Thorpe cabin early Friday afternoon, surveyed the shelves while Jodi peered in from the doorway. He spied a wooden swing Jodi's grandpa made that used to hang from a big oak's limb. A basketball, football, kickball, baseball and bat. Toboggans. He'd agreed to sort out the stuff for Goodwill from the stuff that had seen better days. He'd need to air up a few balls and test for slow leaks.

Jodi smiled. "They loved being surrounded by their grandkids and the children of friends—like you. They'd have been so happy to know that great-grandchildren will be spending time here at the holidays."

Putting the cabin on the market was no doubt on her mind. He knew it weighed on his, and it didn't even belong to his family. If he hadn't had other pressing plans, if the church had wanted to keep him on a permanent basis, maybe he'd buy it himself. Keep it in the family, so to speak. But there was no point in mentioning something that wasn't to be.

On impulse, he grabbed the bright red toboggan that Jodi had been pulling the night he'd discovered her alongside the road. Then he reached for a blue one and stepped out of the shed.

"What do you say we give these babies a test run? Make sure they're still safe for your nieces and nephew?"

"I'll leave that adventure up to you."

"Come on now. The Jodi I knew as a kid would have knocked me into the snow to be the one to make the first run. At least come with me. If I break my neck, I want someone to call 911."

"I can do that."

Together they hiked through the snow up a gentle series of rises behind the cabin. When they finally reached the top of their favorite sledding spot of bygone days, Garrett dropped the toboggans to the ground. Sunshine earlier in the morning had melted the surface snow somewhat, then as the temperature dropped again it refroze into a crusty layer. Not an easy run for beginners, but then they weren't beginners.

"Red or blue?"

"Excuse me? I'm here as a first responder only, remember?"

"We both know you're backing out because you don't think you can beat me down this hill."

She huffed her disagreement. "You think so, do you?"

He straightened both toboggans to face downhill, then lowered himself onto the blue one. "I know so."

She kicked a spray of snow at him, and he ducked. Then, laughing, he adjusted his stocking cap and made himself comfortable, readying for the flight downward. "You're already a poor loser, and you don't even have the guts to give it a shot."

"I don't have anything to prove." She folded her arms as she looked down at him, determined to stand her ground. "I don't want to risk ruining my new coat."

"Sissy."

"Say whatever you want. I'm not doing this."

"Chicken." He made soft clucking sounds, his grin deliberately taunting. That pushed her over the edge.

"Okay, smarty-pants." She grabbed the red toboggan and pulled it a safe distance away from him, then climbed aboard. "We'll see who's laughing hardest when I beat you by a mile."

"Oh, yeah?" He gripped the steering cord as she settled on her toboggan. "Well, Jode, what do you say we make this competition worthwhile. Whoever loses has to eat three pieces of Old Mrs. Bartholomew's fruitcake—without drinking any water."

Jodi made a face. "No way."

"Afraid you'll lose?"

She slanted him a derisive look as her hands tightened on the cord. "You're on."

Satisfied, he grinned again, loving it when the competitive tomboy in Jodi surfaced. "So you're ready?"

"Ready."

"Then…one. Two. Three. Go!"

It took them both a moment to push off, then the toboggans quickly began their descent, picking up speed. He was the heavier of the two, which might have worked to his advantage. But a quick glance in Jodi's direction—at her determined face as she leaned forward and attempted to shift her weight to keep the toboggan on a straight course—told him he wouldn't be coasting over the finish line first if she had anything to say about it.

"Woo-hoo!"

He laughed at her cry of delight as the ponderosas flashed past them in a blur. That icy crust on the snow had them flying now. And it was harder to steer. The wind whipped off his knit cap, chilling his ears, and her hood fell back, freeing her hair to fly behind her in a silky curtain.

Beautiful. But a bump drew his attention back to manning the toboggan beneath him, his gaze focused ahead on the path running by a lightning-struck ponderosa that had always marked the finish line. When from the corner of his peripheral vision, he detected she was losing ground to him, he let out a whoop of triumph—only seconds before Jodi cried out.

"Oh, no!"

He shot a look in her direction, where a slight rise in the course had apparently shifted the trajectory of her toboggan as they neared the homestretch.

She was coming right at him.

Before he could maneuver to escape the inevitable, she plowed into him with enough impact to topple them both into the snow, a jumble of arms and legs.

With snow melting down the back of his neck, he managed to sit up and reach out to Jodi, who'd collapsed across his legs. "You okay, Jodi?"

"I'm sorry, Garrett." Her words came unevenly

as she fought to regain her breath. "I hit a bump and a patch of ice and I couldn't stop it."

"But you're okay?"

His heart hitched as she turned to him, eyes radiant and cheeks flushed, her hair sparkling with snow as if with glittering stardust. She looked more than okay to him.

"Yeah. How about you?"

"It takes more than a pretty woman knocking me off my feet to keep me down." At the uncertain look in her eyes, he jerked his transfixed gaze away. Dumb thing to say. Brothers didn't make a habit of telling sisters they were pretty. Or at least he hadn't told his own sister that much. Not until recently when he knew she could use a boost. "Let's see if we can get ourselves untangled here."

It took several attempts, but with his assistance she was finally able to lift herself off his legs and, freed, he regained his footing, then reached down to clasp her outstretched hand.

"Easy there. Slick here."

She'd barely made it to a standing position when her footing gave way and she pitched forward into his chest, her arms flying around him to stay upright. He managed to remain standing, his hands gripping her upper arms to hold her steady.

And then she looked up at him, eyes wide, her face mere inches from his.

* * *

"I'm sorry…Garrett." To her dismay, her words came out a breathy whisper as she looked at him. Up close, the depths of his stormy gray eyes were even more amazing than she'd remembered.

For a long moment they stared at each other. Was his breath as ragged as hers, his heart pounding a little faster, too? She hadn't been this close to him since she was sixteen. Since that night when…

"Jodi?" he whispered, his head lowering slightly.

Heartbeat accelerating, her gaze dropped to his mouth, then back to his eyes as the moment stretched unbearably. Was he going to kiss her again? Right now?

And then what?

Go tell his buddies like he'd done before, that kissing her was akin to kissing the old family dog? With every ounce of strength she could muster, she pulled abruptly from his arms and stepped back, feeling as dazed as he looked.

"I think I have my footing now. Thanks."

"Uh, sure."

She deliberately looked away, searching for the toboggans where they'd skimmed a number of yards farther down the slope. "So was it a tie? Or are you going to claim victory on grounds of interference?"

Her voice sounded halfway normal. The challenging words of her tomboy self emerging despite feelings far to the contrary of those long-ago days.

Garrett rolled his shoulders as he stuck his gloved fingers down the back of his coat collar and pulled out a fistful of snow. "I was unfairly assaulted in the homestretch. A win was as good as in my pocket, so I hope you enjoy the fruitcake Mrs. B's already delivered to my folks."

"Get real." She trudged toward her toboggan, careful of where she placed her feet. She didn't dare risk him trying to help her up again, even though it had to have been her imagination that he was about to kiss her. Garrett wasn't the type to make the same mistake twice. He'd made it quite clear that kissing her the first time had been a major one.

How dumb was she, anyway?

He jogged a ways up the slope to retrieve his cap, then made his way to his own overturned toboggan. "I suppose we could call it a tie. Or—" He jerked his head in the uphill direction from which they'd come, his gaze challenging. "We could have a rematch."

"In your dreams." She picked up her toboggan. "I'm freezing. You're not the only one who got a collar full of snow. And chicken clucks won't hold any weight this time, so you can keep those to yourself."

He chuckled as he hefted his own toboggan. "Guess we'd better get back to work, then, before Dolly calls out a search-and-rescue team."

"Don't feel obligated. I'm sure you have more than enough to do this close to Christmas. Shut-ins to visit, counseling to do and a Sunday message to prepare."

He popped himself lightly on the forehead with the heel of his hand, then started down the slope, avoiding her gaze. "Thanks for the reminder. I need to give my all to those while I can. They'll soon be a thing of the past."

Struck by the abruptness of his words, she hurried as best she could across the snowy expanse to keep up with him. "What do you mean, a thing of the past?"

"When my contract concludes at the end of the month, I'll be moving on."

Her heart stilled. Dolly and Drew seemed to think Garrett's position was a permanent one. In fact everyone talked as if that was a given. "But I thought—"

"I haven't wanted to say much about it..." He cut her an uncertain glance.

"Are you saying you've turned down a contract? Or do you mean the church isn't extending you one?"

"No contract extension has been offered."

Were the board members crazy? From what she'd seen, Garrett was the best thing that had happened to this church, to the town, in years.

He forced a smile. "It wouldn't matter if they offered one anyway. I came here knowing it was a temporary position, a layover while I prepared for my next phase of ministry. I'd been against coming here in the first place, but my Grandma Jo can be very persuasive."

Why hadn't he said something about this earlier? And why was he telling her now? Because he suspected she'd wanted him to kiss her and had to set things straight? "What are you going to do?"

"Mission work."

She halted, her breath catching as Anton's face flashed through her mind. Then she scurried to again catch up with him as he neared the pine that would have marked the finish line. She tugged on his sleeve and he paused to turn to her. "Outside the country?"

His gaze darkened, as if suspecting she might not approve. "Middle East."

A wave of nausea coursed through her. A dangerous—not a *potentially* dangerous—destination.

"It's been in my heart for years," he continued, "since I first gave my life to God. Now it's time to do something about it."

Now? Right when she hadn't seen him in twelve years and still found herself foolishly harboring a secret hope that maybe they'd both shown up in town at the same time for a reason?

"I'm…happy for you." Was she? Really? The ache in her heart said otherwise. "But I'm shocked your contract isn't being extended. You're so right for this church. From what I hear, you've made a difference in so many lives, bringing young people into active participation and injecting a new energy into the church's ministry."

"Thanks. I'd like to think the past twelve months haven't been in vain."

"They weren't. Which leaves me puzzled as to why you're being let go."

He grinned. "Believe me, Jodi, it's no mystery to me. There's a lot that's gone on behind the scenes that you know nothing about. Not all can look beyond my teen years—the drinking, the pranks, the attitude."

"Randall Moppert?"

"Among others. But for my part, coming under leadership authority has been a struggle at times. I'm learning, but admit I do have a mind of my own. I haven't always done things by the book. Haven't exactly been a poster-child pastor. It hasn't come as a surprise that there's been no talk of a contract renewal."

"But I think a lot of people are expecting you to stay on."

"Which is all the more reason, if you wouldn't mind, to keep this to yourself for the time being. I don't want this parting of ways to cause a division in the church between those who might want me to stay and those who can't get rid of me fast enough. I haven't mentioned it to many, and right now I'd like to focus on what lies ahead and not look back."

"I understand."

All too well, in fact. God had a plan for Garrett's life that clearly didn't include her.

Each lost in thought, they crossed the snowy ground leading to the old shed and put away the toboggans. Then she left Garrett to weed out the sports equipment as she headed back to the cabin and Dolly, her heart heavy.

What if she took Brooke's advice, though, and sought out a position with a new company, decided to work from home—could she perhaps work from Grandma's cabin in Hunter Ridge? There would be no worries about Garrett being her pastor. No reason to confess her relationship with Kel or about the pregnancy or her waffling faith. While Garrett wouldn't hold the former two issues against her, what would a minister do with an old friend whose faith had long ago hiked into the sunset?

* * *

Back in his office late that afternoon, Garrett stared out the window at the lightly falling snow-flakes, unable to focus on his Sunday message preparation.

He'd almost kissed Jodi.

But this time she'd seen it coming and gotten herself out of the way. What was wrong with him? Jodi didn't want her "big brother" kissing her. She hadn't twelve years ago, and she didn't now. Which is why he'd blurted out his plans to leave Hunter Ridge to set her fears at rest.

She seemed taken aback by that news, but it eased the tension-filled atmosphere and diverted his thoughts from how good it had felt to hold her for those brief moments. To gaze into the depths of her eyes, remembering their first kiss and wanting from the very depths of his being to bring about a second.

Fortunately, Jodi's brain had still been func-tioning even if his hadn't been.

"Hey, Garrett, have a minute?"

He looked up to see Sofia standing in the open doorway, Tiana and Leon in the background crowded around Melody's desk, which was cur-rently occupied by Marisela Palmer.

"Come on in." He rose and moved to the seat-ing area, motioning her to sit down. "What's on your mind?"

"I need a man's point of view," she said, lowering her voice as she glanced almost furtively in the direction of Marisela and the kids.

"What's up?"

"Drew."

"Ah." With Sofia, it always had something to do with Drew. He eased himself down into the chair opposite her.

"I learned from Mel Benito, who sometimes serves as an aide to Drew, that Drew's parents will be in Hawaii of all places on Christmas Day. It's a spur-of-the-moment thing—his mom's well-to-do best friend from college lives there now and sent them airline tickets."

"And?"

"I'd like to invite Drew to my folks' place for Christmas dinner." She took a deep breath, then rushed on. "Has your family already invited him?"

"At Hunter's Hideaway, it will be business as usual in the inn's main dining room midday and enjoying a more private affair in the evening. You'd both be welcome to come to that."

"I'm not saying your family needs to invite him. Or me. I was merely wondering if—"

"If he already has plans? His folks being gone is news to me, but I know they're his only family hereabouts since his brother and sister moved away. So all I can say, Sofia, is if you'd like to invite him to your parents' place, do it. Now. Once word gets out that he's on his own for the holiday, he'll be inundated with invitations."

"I know." Her mouth took a downward turn. "Every unmarried woman within miles will be calling him. Their mothers and grandmothers, too."

"Make yourself one of them, then. The first."

Her forehead creased. "But what if he says yes to my invitation, then someone he'd rather spend the day with calls later? He'd be stuck with me."

Garrett frowned. "Sofia Ramos, no man in his right mind would consider spending time with you as being stuck. Trust me on this."

"I don't want to look pushy like a few of the other women."

"He won't think it's pushy. I imagine he'll appreciate joining a family for the day. I've seen him around your kids, and he seems to enjoy them."

She rose to her feet, a determined look on her face. "Okay, then, I'll do it."

"Don't delay."

When she and her children departed, he moved again to stare out the window. *Open Drew's eyes, Lord.* When had his buddy gotten so thickheaded about women that he couldn't see what was right in front of him?

Of course, he should talk. Except for a short-lived relationship with river-running cohort Bena Darden that ended disappointingly when she couldn't deal with the U-turn his life took after Drew's accident, few women he'd dated since the night he'd kissed Jodi measured up. He'd gotten himself stuck, for whatever reason, in some teenage time warp. Probably, just like Drew, he'd obliviously passed up a dozen women who'd have made exceptional life partners.

After coming close to kissing Jodi today, it was definitely time to get a grip and move on.

Chapter Ten

"Your family arrives when, Jodi?" At the conclusion of Sunday's worship service, Marisela rose from the pew beside her. "Christmas Eve?"

"Actually, the day before that, although my sisters' husbands will drive up on Christmas Eve."

"I know you're looking forward to seeing all of them."

She was—and she wasn't.

She'd been in Hunter Ridge a week now, and she'd accomplished so little that she'd intended to get done. Even with Dolly pitching in and with Garrett's occasional assistance, the place was in no way ready to put on the market. This week, too, she needed to make further headway on the Christmas project, submit an online application to Brooke's new company, and somehow get the house readied for a family gathering—

one that would make a lasting memory for her nieces and nephew.

"It's been a year since I've seen them," Jodi couldn't help adding wistfully. "It's a good thing my sisters send photos or I probably wouldn't even recognize the kids."

"Your grandmother certainly would have loved that you're all getting together. Just like old times."

"She would."

Marisela nodded toward the front of the church as chatting people secured coats and headed toward the doors, eager to get to a noontime meal. "Wasn't Garrett's message good this morning? That young man is exactly what this stagnating congregation needed. I foresee a bright future for Christ's Church."

Obviously it hadn't crossed her mind that church leaders were thinking otherwise.

"Yes, a very good message." And it had been. Given that he hadn't even started on it when he'd left following their toboggan run, it was especially amazing. Another clear indicator to her that Garrett's God-given gifts were being put to good use here. But who was she to say God didn't have a plan for him elsewhere?

Marisela's husband, Bert, leaned in. "Would you like to join some of us for lunch again? We'll be heading to the Log Cabin Café."

"Thanks. I'd love to, but there are quite a few things I need to see to. Time is flying by so quickly."

"Don't drive yourself too hard. That's one of the dangers of our modern holiday season. No time to stop and smell the Christmas tree. You don't want to overdo and come down with one of those colds that are going around."

She sure couldn't afford to get sick. Although, if she came down with a cold, that might keep her sisters and their offspring at bay...

When she stepped out into the bright sunshine, amazed at how quickly the snow was melting from the sidewalks and parking lot, she couldn't help but notice the chatting cluster of people surrounding Garrett. His cousin Grady with a woman Jodi presumed to be his fiancée, Sunshine. A couple she remembered as his Uncle Dave and Aunt Elaine, the latter whom she'd heard was battling breast cancer. Drew, too. And *Sofia*, of course.

It seemed every time she turned around, a smiling Sofia was at Garrett's side. Which made her imaginings of Garrett's intention to kiss her a few days ago seem even more absurd. Of course he hadn't been about to kiss her after they'd collided on the snowy slope. Why would he settle for his tomboy childhood playmate when a perfect pastor's—or missionary's—wife always appeared to be hovering at his elbow?

Petite. Feminine. Soft-spoken. She was a musically gifted and culinarily talented woman with two sweet children who would tug at any man's heartstrings.

Jodi altered her course to give the grouping a wide berth, but had just reached her pickup when Garrett jogged up.

"Hey, Jode. Have a minute?"

She held up an index finger. "One."

"Then let me make good use of it."

He glanced back at family and friends who were still visiting with each other, and Jodi caught Sofia's lingering look in their direction before she turned again to Drew.

"What's up?"

"That load of wood I promised? Sorry I haven't gotten back with it yet. My sermon prep wasn't coming easy yesterday and time got away from me. I figured you wouldn't appreciate me banging around out back at eleven o'clock at night."

"No, I wouldn't have. But the time you took for the morning's message paid off. So no complaints here."

"You liked it?"

"I did." But once again, the words of his message had hit their unintended target. Or at least unintended by Garrett. God might have had a hand in hitting the bull's-eye painted on her heart, though. Why was it so hard to believe, as Garrett had shared, that God wanted His children to forgive themselves, just as He had forgiven them?

"Anyway," Garrett continued, "if it's okay with you, I'll swing by this afternoon and drop off the firewood."

"Whatever's convenient, but you may want to bring someone along to help unload and stack." *Sofia, maybe?* "I'll be out most of the afternoon."

He raised a brow in query, but she didn't feel inclined to explain her planned run to Canyon Springs while the roads were clear. She'd thoroughly explored Hunter Ridge last week, trying to find a replacement for Grandma's missing baby Jesus, but to no avail. A few phone calls to the neighboring town, however, turned up a possibility at a little gift shop that was part of a hotel and restaurant there. Kit's Lodge.

"I can do that." He scuffed the toe of his shoe in a crusty patch of snow. "So…do you have your tom all picked out?"

"Tom?"

"Tom turkey. For Christmas dinner. Grandma always says one day of refrigerator thawing for every four pounds, so keep that in mind. A twenty or twenty-five pounder for that crew you're expecting could take five or six days—or more."

She laughed. Who did he think he was talking with here, Rachael Ray? "I'm not cooking a turkey. You know me better than that."

He clasped his hand to his heart. "I thought you were supposed to be delivering a Christmas just like your grandma used to give you and your sisters."

"I did come across her roasted butternut squash recipe. One for corn-bread dressing, too. And ginger apple cranberry sauce. But if I'm not messing with a home-cooked turkey, I don't see any point in burning the kitchen down trying to make side dishes or risk an ER run for family-wide food poisoning. My sisters can live with catering from Diamond's grocery store. After all, when I was back for Christmas last year, we all went out to a nice restaurant. The kids won't know the difference."

"Are you kidding me? That kind of substitution borders on sacrilegious."

She shrugged. No doubt Sofia could fix a turkey with one hand tied behind her back. Probably homemade rolls, too. And mashed potatoes without lumps. "Christmas dinner is all about people, right? And Jesus, of course. You know what the Bible has to say about those whose god is their stomach. Road to destruction and all that."

"I think you're taking that out of context."

"So sue me." She opened the driver's-side door and slid in behind the steering wheel.

"This isn't over, Jodi. You owe it to those kids to give them a real taste of old-fashioned Christmas."

"Not. Going. To. Happen." She pulled the door closed and started up the engine, unable to keep a straight face at Garrett's look of dismay. With a cheerful wave, she backed out of the parking space and headed off for lunch and a bit of shopping in Canyon Springs.

But she couldn't help but look in her rearview mirror as he stood there starting after her, then abruptly turned away and strode back to Drew... and Sofia.

Jodi was having Christmas dinner catered.

Garrett stacked a final armful of split, seasoned wood in an iron rack located not too far from the back porch of her grandparents' place. Close enough to bring a few logs inside as needed, but not close enough to harbor bugs and critters that might like to slip inside the cozy cabin.

Catered. That was almost blasphemous in small-town America, wasn't it? She'd made reference to a kitchen burning and food poisoning, but surely she was underrating her culinary skills. She'd been living on her own for years back in Philly. Surely she hadn't existed solely on cream cheese, pretzels and cheesesteak.

Jodi was messing with him. That's all.

He returned to the back of his SUV a few more times, hauling the remaining armfuls of wood to the side porch to get things started when Jodi's family arrived. Generously donated by his folks, the entire load was a bit more than needed for the following week. He covered the larger stacked pile with a canvas tarp to keep the wood dry, then, back at the SUV, he shook wood chips out of the heavy plastic sheet with which he'd lined the back interior, rearranged things neatly, and secured the tailgate.

He glanced at his watch. Four thirty. Not too much longer and the sun would set, but no sign of Jodi. Where'd she gotten off to? Not that it was any of his business. But the temperature was dropping, and from the looks of the sky, another snow system might be moving in. Big brothers had to look out for little sisters.

He bit back a groan. Little sister. Right.

As he opened the driver's-side door, he glanced back at the cabin. A lot of good memories had been made here. He could see why Star and Ronda wanted to share them with their kids before the place sold. Why they counted on Aunt Jodi to make it happen.

Yeah, Jodi was just messing with him with all that talk of catering Christmas dinner. She had every intention of pulling out all the stops for her nieces and nephew but, Jodi-like, was giving him a hard time.

Shaking his head, he climbed into his vehicle and fastened his seat belt, unable to suppress a grin at how she'd had him going.

But just in case it wasn't all talk, he'd better come up with a backup plan…

Jodi came home empty-handed.

The baby Jesus of a size similar to her grandma's set sold out before she got there. When she'd called on Saturday, the person she'd talked to hadn't been inclined to sell any of the nativity pieces separately. After all, what other customer would want to purchase a crèche without the star of the show? She'd have had to buy the entire set, which she'd been prepared to do. But with three still in stock, she hadn't had the foresight to ask them to hold one for her.

At least Kit's Lodge offered a fabulous Sunday menu and, when a very pregnant Kara Kenton and her husband, Trey, saw her coming out of the adjoining gift shop, they invited her to join them for lunch. Kara said their church was still receiving generous donations, so hopefully—even if Christ's Church fell short—there would be more than enough when they combined their projects.

But now on Monday morning, Jodi was back to searching the cabin for the missing baby Jesus.

She couldn't have the kids racing down the stairs on Christmas Day to an empty manger. That would give them a memorable Christmas, all right. Jesus a no-show.

But where had He gotten off to?

Once again she emptied out the box that held the crèche and figurines, the pieces now arranged on the console table, but with no success. Maybe she'd find Him in one of the other decoration boxes. But even though she and Dolly had thoroughly cleaned the bedrooms and main room, she wasn't ready to drag out all the holiday trappings to look. She didn't even have a Christmas tree for the kids yet. Star and Ronda wanted a live tree like Grandma always had—one with a root ball that could be planted on the property in the spring, which meant a trip to the local landscape nursery.

Wandering into the kitchen, she looked down at her lengthy to-do list on the countertop and shook her head. She'd known she'd be busy getting the cabin ready to put on the market, but where were the hours she'd hoped to fill with quiet contemplation? Time to weigh the pros and cons of relocating overseas or leaving Smith-Smith altogether. Time to finally come to terms with the impact Kel, Anton and her unborn child were having on her life.

Time to get right with God.

In all honesty, though, despite the initial confusion that had dogged her on the flight to Phoenix and the shuttle ride up the mountain, the choice to leave the company she'd worked for the past five years now seemed like a no-brainer. Submitting that application to the new company tonight would be one decision off her mental checklist. Only one hundred more to go.

If she worked hard and stayed focused, maybe she could get the project donations finalized and things ready by Wednesday evening for her family's arrival. Thursday afternoon would be spent with volunteers to wrap the donations, but she'd have Thursday morning mostly to herself. A long walk in the woods appealed, or maybe time in front of a crackling fire with a cup of hot cocoa. She needed time to catch her breath before her family descended on her.

At the sound of a familiar tune, she reached for her cell phone. Garrett. One more thing she hadn't bargained on when returning to town—renewing a teenage heartbreak.

"Hey, Jodi. Did you see I got the firewood delivered yesterday?"

"I did. I was going to call and thank you." Just not right away. She needed to put more distance between them. "I have someone coming to inspect and clean the fireplace chimney today. Then I'll bring in the logs and have it all ready to light when my family walks through the door on Friday."

"Good deal." There was a long pause, which she didn't rush to fill. "Will you be coming in to the church today? A few folks dropped off baby stuff after yesterday's worship service. They set it just inside the door of my office, but I can move it to the storeroom if you'd like."

"Thanks." She couldn't avoid Garrett forever, but the fewer one-on-one encounters they had, the better her aching heart would feel.

"When do you plan to get your volunteers together to wrap and label the packages?"

"Thursday afternoon. Then delivery to Canyon Springs Christian on Friday morning."

"I may ride along with you ladies. I can do any heavy lifting, and there are a few things I'd like to talk over with the pastor there. Jason Kenton's served as a mentor of sorts since I took on this interim position."

Jason was also a young man holding a responsible church leadership role in a town in which she understood he'd spent his teen years and who had probably dealt with challenges similar to Garrett's. Undoubtedly Garrett had shared his plan for mission work with Jason, just as he would have with Drew.

She'd need to show more interest in that. Ask more questions. But not now. She wanted to get off the phone and back to her never-ending list. Find a tree. Shop for more grab-bag gifts and a gender-neutral present to be drawn by one of the adults. Place the Christmas dinner order at Diamond's grocery.

And that was just the bare beginnings of what stretched ahead of her before she'd be ready for Christmas Day.

"Jodi? You there?" Garrett's voice drew her back to the present.

"Yeah. I'm here. Just have a lot on my mind— and my to-do list."

"Well, then, I'd better let you get back to it. I still need to stop by, though, to replace those old smoke alarms. When did you say the chimney guy is coming? I could time my visit for when he's there."

"She. Chimney gal. And I'm not sure when she'll be arriving. We kind of left it open-ended for when she can work me into her schedule."

"Okay...I'll see what I can figure out."

Poor Garrett. Jumping through hoops not to be in the company of a lone woman. Maybe that's why things hadn't progressed more rapidly with Sofia? How *did* a single pastor get one-on-one time with a potential mate, anyway? While she'd rather not have him drop by today, she took mercy on him. "I can call you when she lets me know she's on her way."

"You'd do that?" The relief in his voice was evident. "I have the new alarms and a stepladder, so I'm all ready to go."

"Don't forget to bring me the receipt so I can reimburse you."

"Yes, ma'am!"

No doubt had she been able to see him, she'd have caught a brisk salute. "See you later, then."

"You, too."

But for a long moment, neither hung up, the silence between them stretching uncomfortably. It was as though he wanted to say something more—and she was expecting him to.

"Bye," he finally offered.

"Bye."

Then the line went dead.

Chapter Eleven

Garrett secured a new smoke detector in the ceiling of the second bedroom, thankful he'd thought to check them out earlier. Timing this chore with the chimney sweep's visit had worked out well.

"How's it going?"

He glanced down at Jodi standing in the doorway, and his heart did a betraying tap dance. In a pair of fitted bib overalls and a long-sleeved emerald T-shirt, her hair pulled back in a long braid, she looked bright and perky this afternoon. She'd made herself scarce since his arrival. Whether avoiding him or attending to other more pressing matters, he couldn't be sure. If it was the former, though, he had only himself to blame for that near-miss kiss. No wonder she seemed skittish around him.

He descended the ladder. "Just about done."

"Kriss is coming along with the chimney, too.

It's taking longer than she thought it would. I guess it's been quite a few years since the folks had it cleaned out."

"Good to get it attended to, then. All safe for your family's arrival."

She nodded, then started to turn away.

"Jodi?"

She paused. "Yeah?"

What could he say to her that would ease the awkwardness between them? He sure couldn't tell her how he felt about her. How he'd felt about her since he was eighteen. Not a cool confession coming from someone she thought of as a big brother. Blurting that out would only further distance her.

"Um, never mind."

Something akin to disappointment flickered through her eyes. What had she hoped he'd say? That he valued her in the same way he did his younger sister? That everything was exactly as it had been between them as kids?

But he wasn't about to lie.

Which left him with nothing to say.

She nodded, then disappeared down the hallway to return to the main rooms. He carefully folded the stepladder, gathered up his tools and tossed the decrepit smoke alarm into the box with the others. When he'd made a few trips out to his SUV to secure his equipment, he returned to the cabin where Jodi was sorting through items she'd pulled from the cabinets and drawers and spread out on the kitchen counter.

Her nose wrinkling, she held up one item and waved it at him. A blue plastic device with a handle on one end and an oval-shaped opening on the other. "I don't even know what this is."

He approached to take it from her, unable to suppress a smile as he turned it over in his hands. Then he reached for an unopened glass container of jelly. "This, my dear girl, is a jar opener. You place the little lip under the rim of the lid like this, then lift it up like that and—" A soft popping sound confirmed the seal had been broken. "Voilà!"

He easily unscrewed and lifted the lid.

Her expression brightened. "Grandma was a sucker for those gizmo catalogs and kitchen shops."

He surveyed the items on the countertop. "It does seem she has a showroom's worth of gadgets right here."

"You're getting ready to leave?"

"Need to be on my way."

"Do you think I could get your help with one more thing?" She made a hopeful little face. "I don't want to take advantage of your time, but when I was up in the attic where the kids will be sleeping, I noticed it's really cold up there. Outside air seems to be creeping in around the windows."

"Let's take a look."

"Kriss?" Jodi called to the woman who was barely visible in the fireplace's yawning opening. "I'll be right back."

A muffled response indicated her announcement had been heard, then they headed to the narrow staircase that led to the space above.

"See what I mean?" Jodi briskly rubbed her hands up and down her arms when they reached the top. The space was in reality a finished room extending the length of the cabin, where it was possible to stand upright and dormer windows let in adequate light and fresh air, but her grandparents had always called it the attic because of the slanting ceilings. "Even in sleeping bags on cots, I can't put the kids up here with the wind whistling in around the windows like that."

"It is a tad on the chilly side." He moved to one of the dormer window recessions to inspect it, surprised at the force of the cold air squeezing in around the edges of the window when he held his hands out to it.

"Pretty bad, isn't it?" Jodi slipped in beside him, her hands outstretched to the window as well. "There isn't enough time to get it replaced, is there?"

As her arm brushed his, the fresh scent of her shampoo filling his senses, he pulled slightly away. "Maybe not, but I think I can do a temporary fix for you."

"Would you?"

Still a little too close, he stepped back from the dormer nook, not wanting a repeat performance of last week's temptation, then moved to the other window. She followed behind him.

It was the same story on the draft at that window. "I may have something in my vehicle that will do the trick. I helped Dolly and Al with winterizing their place."

So why was he standing there looking at her instead of hustling off to get the needed supplies? A slant of afternoon sunlight reflected off the polished hardwood floor, illuminating her with a golden glow. Every fiber of his body cried out to take her in his arms, to tell her how he felt about her.

"Is something wrong?"

"We've been friends a long time, Jodi."

Her forehead wrinkled at that out-of-the-blue statement. "Yes, we have."

"So maybe you should get someone else to fix the windows." Oh, wow, that made a lot of sense.

She gave him a look that confirmed she was doubting his sanity. "Okaaay."

"It's just that—"

What good would it do to try to explain? Anything he said would only make her more uncomfortable around him. And he sure didn't want her to feel sorry for him. But maybe she needed to understand why he'd be pulling back as soon as he got these windows taken care of, that while it was great to see her again, he wasn't feeling especially brotherly toward her right now. But a confession like that would be sure to send her running for the hills.

"Something's wrong. Talk to me, Garrett."

He drew in a breath, determined to make something up and get out of the house as fast as he could. That is, until she stepped forward to place her hand on his arm and his gaze melted into hers.

"I don't want to make you uncomfortable, Jodi, but—" He placed his hand atop hers where it still rested on his arm. "I know you've always thought of me as a big brother. And I know I offended you years ago when I cornered you in the mudroom that night and, well, didn't treat you as a big brother should."

He heard her quick intake of breath at his confession as her gaze remained locked on his.

"I…wasn't offended."

"Maybe *offended* is too strong of a word. But you were caught off guard. Embarrassed at your grandma walking in on us. Upset at my betrayal of our friendship enough to avoid me at church that night." She was looking at him as if he'd lost what was left of his mind. But he plunged on, determined to clear the air. "I should have asked your forgiveness when you first arrived here last week, gotten this out in the open. But there didn't seem to be an appropriate time."

Here goes, Lord. "What I'm trying to say is… I'm apologizing now so that you can understand why I—"

Jodi tightened her grip on his arm, cutting him off. "I didn't avoid you at the Christmas Eve service, Garrett."

"No? When I looked for you afterward, started to approach you in the parking lot where you were heading to your grandma's car, you looked straight through me like I didn't exist. Just kept on walking. You clearly didn't want to speak to me."

He'd come after her even after saying those hurtful things to his friends? Why? But she hadn't seen him looking for her in the parking lot. Maybe she'd been in shock.

"Then you never contacted me again," he continued, "even though I'd given you my email address earlier in the day. I didn't blame you for not feeling the same way about me as I'd come to feel about you. But I felt awful that I'd overstepped the bounds of a friendship that meant a lot to me."

He was claiming he'd had romantic feelings for her? Feelings he didn't think she reciprocated?

No, he was putting a spin on it that flew in the face of what really happened. Her jaw hardened as she stepped away from him.

"Kissing Jodi," she recited quietly, "would be about as thrilling as kissing our Labrador retriever."

He stared at her as realization dawned. Realization that his selective memory of that night—attempting now to convince her that the kiss they'd shared had meant something to him—wasn't going to fly.

"Yes," she continued, "I overheard you sharing that tender sentiment with your buddies. It elicited the laughs I'm sure you were looking for."

"Jodi, I—" He shook his head slowly as he reached for her hand.

She pulled away as the memories of that long-ago night slammed into her with surprising force. But she wouldn't cry. She'd shed those silent tears into her pillow years ago, hiding them from her family.

"Please don't say anything more, Garrett. That evening is one I don't care to relive." She turned toward the door, but he moved to block her way.

"Hear me out. Please?"

"Then have the decency to be honest, Garrett. Stop with the spin. It's not becoming for a man of God."

"I wasn't spinning, Jodi. When you came back

to town that Christmas, my let's-be-buddies conviction crumbled. It scared me to death. But without giving you any warning, I acted on my feelings when the opportunity presented itself. That's when I kissed you."

"Please don't try to convince me it meant anything to you."

"But it did. It *did*."

"And the Labrador thing?"

He drew in a breath, his eyes pleading. "The guys were all noticing you. Richard was even wagering on who could steal a kiss first. I couldn't let that happen." He reached for her hand again and this time captured it. "Believe me, the kiss we shared meant something to me. It still does."

The kiss had meant something to her once, too. Before it had been overshadowed by her grandma's scolding and Garrett's callous words to his friends.

"But I immediately realized," he continued, his hand tightening on hers, "that you weren't in the same place I was. You were only sixteen and still thinking of me as your pal. A big brother. So I didn't attempt to contact you."

"Brother?" She gave him an incredulous look. "I'd had the world's biggest crush on you for years. Do you think I'd return your kiss the way I did if I thought of you as my *brother*? Think again."

"But you looked so shocked. And then afterward—"

"I *was* shocked—as in surprised. Stunned. Dazed. And Grandma barging in on us was embarrassing. But I wasn't offended or upset—until by your own words you made it clear that the kiss meant nothing to you. That it was a big joke."

"I had no idea you'd overheard that." His eyes filled with what appeared to be genuine remorse. "It was a dumb thing to say. A desperate attempt to run the other guys off. I'm sorry."

"You expect me to believe after all this time that you didn't regret kissing me?"

"I did regret it, Jodi." He gently tugged on her hand to draw her closer, but his words cut deep as they confirmed her long-held belief. "I regretted it—but only because I'd betrayed your trust in me. And—" his words came softly, his gaze intent "—I regretted that I'd never be given the opportunity to kiss you again."

"Garrett—" This was too much, too fast. Her head was spinning as she tried to comprehend what he was telling her.

Before she could protest, he cupped her face in his hands. "So unless you have any objections, claiming that second kiss is exactly what I'm going to do."

She stared into his eyes—so full of hope. Garrett had cared for her? Cared for her more than as a little sister? But she shouldn't let him kiss her now. Too much time had passed. Too many unshared secrets darkened her heart. And he was leaving soon for a dangerous destination. A kiss now would be unwise. Complicate things.

And yet…slowly she shook her head, unable to voice a coherent objection. That's all the encouragement he needed, for he closed his eyes and leaned in to gently touch his lips to hers.

Garrett. Deliberately shoving away the nagging concerns, her own eyes closed as she drank in the amazing sensation of his mouth on hers. Felt his fingers lightly caress her jaw. Breathed in the faint scent of his aftershave. The chill of the room and the whistling of the wind coming in around the windows faded in the warmth of his touch.

Surely *this* kiss meant something to him.

His hands moved to her waist, and she slipped her arms around his neck, drawing even closer as if neither ever wanted the moment to end. A murmur of hope bubbled up in her spirit as his mouth again captured hers. Was she really being held in Garrett's arms, the future taking on an unexpected brilliance as new doors opened?

"Jodi," Garrett murmured against her ear. "I—"

A loud, merry tune abruptly shattered the quiet, startling her. The cell phone in her pocket.

Garrett grazed his lips along her cheek, then reluctantly stepped back.

With his arms no longer around her, the room's chill once again pierced and, dazed from the unexpected turn of events, she pulled out her phone. Star.

"I'd better take this. It's my sister. Keep your fingers crossed that they've changed their minds about coming."

He nodded, and she longed to reach out to him, but he moved away to again inspect a dormer window.

She forced a cheery note into her voice. "Hey, Star, what's up?"

"I wanted to let you know there's been a change in plans."

Jodi's spirits soared. "That's too bad."

"No, it's not. Ronda and I will be bringing the kids up on Wednesday instead of Friday. That way we can all have more time to relax and visit, and the kids will get more snow time. The weather forecast looks promising for additional white stuff."

Jodi's skyrocketing hopes deflated. There went any hoped-for time alone—and time to spend with Garrett to come to terms with what had just happened between them. "There's no way I can be ready for you by Wednesday."

"Don't worry about it. Ronda and I'll be there

to help now, so don't knock yourself out. We got to thinking that we're dumping a lot on you. Expecting you to make all this happen for our kids, and that's not exactly fair."

No it wasn't, but… "I don't even have a tree yet."

The porch rails had to be wrapped in fresh greenery and fairy lights, too. An order for Christmas dinner needed to be placed, groceries bought. More gifts purchased. Activities planned.

Baby Jesus found.

"Star, I'm not nearly done clearing things out and boxing them up for keeping or a drop-off at Goodwill."

"Since we're coming early," Star said cheerfully, obviously thinking they'd hit on the ideal solution with an early arrival, "we can help with all that. And we won't take no for an answer. We'll pick up fried chicken or subs when we get to town, so don't plan anything for lunch, okay?"

Jodi glanced toward Garrett, who was watching her with sympathy in his eyes, obviously getting the gist of the conversation. What choice did she have but to agree with her sisters' plans? "Okay. Guess I'll see you then."

"Count on it."

When her sister hung up, Jodi re-pocketed her cell phone.

"Not what you wanted to hear, was it?" Garrett moved to stand beside her.

"No. As I'm sure you could tell from my side of the conversation, my sisters and their kids are coming early. So I have until noon Wednesday to get everything done that I have to get done."

"I'll help as much as I can. And I'll start with these windows."

"Thanks." But the heaviness in her heart didn't dissipate despite the opportunity to spend more time with Garrett. "I really needed—"

Time alone with God.

"We'll get 'er done, Jodi." He reached for her hand and lifted it to his lips for quick kiss. "And while we're working together—"

"We have things we need to talk about," she finished.

"Right."

But she wasn't sure she wanted to talk about them. To dissect and pull apart the blissful moments she'd just spent in Garrett's arms. To come back down to a world of reality—Garrett's imminent departure and her secrets that would have to be shared if things were to move ahead between them.

"Or maybe," she ventured, "we just live with knowing that we were stupid teenagers and that God knew what He was doing back then when

He kept us apart. Not try to make something happen outside of His will that He has no intention of placing His blessing on."

Chapter Twelve

Garrett flinched inwardly at her words as he thoughtfully stroked her hand with his thumb. Was she right? Were the kisses they'd shared only a few moments ago merely a rebound from their teenage years, holding no substance? "Is that what you want? To set aside what just happened between us?"

"A lot of years have passed. We're different people than we were back then."

"True. We're now adults who are fully capable of honestly discussing our feelings. Capable of listening to each other and listening to God." He gently squeezed her hand. "I know the timing stinks with me readying to leave town, and I can't tell you what the future will bring. I can't tell you what God's plans are for my life, let alone yours. But I do know I'm open to whatever time He needs to share with us His direction. Are you?"

"I—" Her eyes searched his uncertainly. Searching—for what? A guarantee? A promise he couldn't make at this time? "I…am."

He softly released a pent-up breath he didn't know he'd been holding.

"But—" she hurried on before he could speak, "there are things you don't know about me, Garrett. Things that will make you feel much differently about me. Things that will open your eyes to the fact that maybe God has already cast His vote against any future for us."

What was she talking about? "Sometimes we let things get bigger in our minds than they really are, forgetting there's nothing that God can't make right."

"He can't take me back in time to make better choices."

"No, but—"

"I got pregnant, Garrett," she blurted, pulling her hands away from his and taking a step back. "About a year after I moved to Philadelphia, I had a relationship with a man I wasn't married to. And… I got pregnant."

A muscle tightened in his throat.

Anton? Or some other guy? But he couldn't point accusing fingers at her extramarital relationship. He, too, was guilty as charged. But she didn't have a child now…did she? Was she trying to tell him she'd had an abortion? "So…you have a child?"

She shook her head, and his gut tightened.

"No. Not a full-term baby. I miscarried him— or her—at three months. Four years ago this very month."

Grateful she hadn't made a decision to end a life, but not relieved when he saw the raw pain in her eyes, he again took her hand in both of his. "I'm sorry."

"And you know what's even worse? What still eats me alive at times?" She blinked back tears. "For most of those three months once I suspected I was pregnant, I woke up every single morning and went to bed every single night wishing that baby away. Wishing from the depths of my soul that I'd dreamed the nightmare it had become during my every waking moment. Shaking my fist at God because He'd allowed it to happen."

Chin trembling, she hung her head.

"I didn't want that baby, Garrett. Not…not until only a few days before I lost him. I'd just begun to come to terms with my reality, with the fact that I carried a precious *life* within me when, suddenly, something went wrong."

She looked at him again, her dark eyes filled with anguish.

"Did God," she continued, "answer my prayers to put that baby out of my life? I don't know, but

I'll always wonder. Wonder what impact on the world that life might have had if I'd carried him to full term. I mean, even though the situations are quite different, what if Mary, the mother of Jesus, had panicked and rejected him the way I rejected my own child? Prayed his little unborn life away?"

Staring into her pleading eyes, his mind flashed to her reaction when they'd first discovered her grandma's nativity set was missing baby Jesus. How he'd unknowingly persuaded her to work on a project for unwed mothers.

"Oh, Jodi." His heart breaking, he gently tugged her forward.

She came willingly, slipping her arms around his waist to press the side of her face against his chest. To cling to him as though somehow she could draw strength from him as her tears flowed quietly, her body trembling in his arms.

His sweet, sweet Jodi had made a wrong choice—and borne so much pain as a result. He closed his eyes and laid his head against hers. *Please, God, hold her tighter than I can. Heal her heart. Fill her with your peace. Give me the words of comfort she needs to hear.*

The cold coming in around the windows seemed to intensify, the silence around them broken only by the sound of Jodi's muffled grief. Had the chimney sweep finished up by now?

Left already? He'd gladly bear any consequences should someone take an exception to him being here alone with Jodi. She needed him, and he wouldn't turn her away.

Right now he only wanted to comfort and protect—for a lifetime—the woman he held so closely. A woman he'd so swiftly grown to care for—to love? Plans for the mission field threatened to fade into the background. But he'd made a commitment. To God, if not to a missions team itself yet. A commitment he still had every intention of fulfilling. But was it his Heavenly Father's plan to wrench this woman from his heart—or to somehow work things out between them?

He tightened his arms around her. How long they remained standing in the upstairs room, entwined in each other's arms, he couldn't have told. Time stood still. But eventually, Jodi pulled slightly back and looked up at him, lashes starred with tears. "Thank you, Garrett."

He leaned in to kiss her forehead. "You're forgiven, Jodi. You know God's already done that, don't you? From the moment you first cried out to Him."

She nodded, wiping away a tear, and he handed her his handkerchief. "But it's hard for me to forgive myself."

"At the risk of sounding blunt, being unwilling

to forgive yourself is kind of like taking Jesus's sacrificial gift and tossing it in the trash."

"But I've harbored such a deep-seated anger toward God about all of it. Anger because He didn't stop me from getting involved with Kel. Anger because I lost my baby. Anger because of Anton's death."

"Is that why things didn't work out between the two of you? You told him about the baby and he couldn't accept it?"

"No. Even though he wanted to marry me, I couldn't bring myself to tell him. I couldn't even tell the baby's father. Nobody knew except me, my doctor and the medical staff. Not even my family."

She'd borne her grief alone.

"But—but can't you see, Garrett, that I'm not exactly front-runner material for you, as a pastor, to be getting involved with? You may be able to forgive my past mistakes, but you can't partner with someone who's held a grudge against God, whose faith is still as wobbly as a sapling in the wind."

He gently cupped her face in his hand. "We're called believers for a reason, Jodi. Believers in God. Believers that He loves us and has good plans for us. Start believing now, this very moment, putting your confidence and trust in Him again. Let this be a turning point in your life that you'll look back on and be thankful for."

"You make it sound so simple."

"We make it more complicated than it is. I know you've often heard that without faith it's impossible to please God. We have to believe He exists and recognize He rewards those of us who seek Him." He smiled encouragingly. "And when you decide to believe—it's a *choice*, Jodi—it's been my experience that your eyes will be opened to how God has been with you all along. And you'll begin to see evidence of His continued presence reinforced, even in the midst of the worst of heartaches."

Hadn't God found him when he was wallowing in the lowest moments of his life following Drew's injury?

"So what do you say, Jodi?" He had no right to ask her this, not with his future up in the air. But he couldn't stop himself. "Are you willing to join me in not only renewing your belief in Him, but believing He'll provide us answers to where He wants our friendship to go?"

Her eyes searched his. "Kinda scary, isn't it? I mean, what if He says no?"

"If he does, then we can know He has our best in mind and have peace with that." He could say that glibly enough, but deep down he knew what he wanted. Knew he'd be deeply disappointed if

God permanently closed the door. "So…I'll ask you again. Are you willing to step out with me to see what He has in mind?"

A multitude of thoughts were obviously racing through her head. Then she swallowed. Nodded. "I am."

Joy bolted through him. But he'd just leaned in, hoping for a kiss to seal their pact, when from somewhere above their heads came a loud thump. Then a scrambling, scraping sound.

Jodi's eyes widened. "What's that?"

"Up on the housetop, reindeer pause…?" he couldn't help but sing softly.

She gently punched his arm. "Oh, you."

He laughed. "I think our chimney sweep has moved to the roof. Should we go out and make sure she's okay?"

"Maybe we'd better."

Hand-in-hand they headed to the stairs, his heart filled with hope. But uncertainty lingered under the surface for, as Jodi had put it, how would God cast His vote?

For the remainder of the day and all through the next, Jodi's heart sang as she went about her chores. Praise songs bubbled up within. Old hymns surfaced from childhood that she'd long forgotten. And deep down inside, a peace she hadn't had in years flooded her soul. No, there were no guarantees that God had a plan for her and Garrett as a couple, but her joy went much deeper than the glimmering hope she held for that.

Today, all on her own, she'd made a gift delivery to Kimmy, a local fifteen-year-old girl seven months pregnant, who'd recently been kicked out of her home. An elderly great-aunt getting by on Social Security had taken her in, so the two were struggling even though determined to give the baby up to a family who would love and care for it. Jodi had found herself encouraged by the girl's resolve not to allow a mistake to become an even deeper, more permanent tragedy. And to her surprise, for the first time ever, when accusing fingers began to point at Jodi in her imagination, she'd prayerfully pushed them aside. Somehow, she hadn't come away from an encounter with the pregnant young woman with self-condemnation filling her *own* heart.

She'd never before confessed to anyone the full nature of her relationship with Kel or the loss of her unborn child. There had never before been an opportunity to be held in comforting arms as the grief of regrets and loss poured out freely. Never had she confessed her carefully hidden doubts as to God's love for her. Until Garrett.

It was long overdue. She could see that now.

And to audibly hear Garrett pronounce with

such assurance that God had forgiven her? It had been as if a dam inside her soul broke open, and for the first time in ever so long, she was no longer held hostage to her doubts and fears.

O come all ye faithful...!

"We're making progress." Not long before sunset on Tuesday, Garrett stepped back to admire the fairy lights he'd finished wrapping around the greenery on the porch railings.

From the open cabin doorway, Dolly nodded her approval. "Picture-perfect, don't you think, Jodi?"

"So festive," she agreed. The tiny lights sparkling in the twilight reflected the glow in her heart—and the telltale shine in Garrett's eyes when he looked at her.

"If you have everything done out here," his landlady said as she motioned to the interior of the cabin behind her, "there's tomato soup and grilled cheese sandwiches awaiting you. Better get in there before Al eats more than his fair share."

Once inside, Jodi was again filled with a deep sense of satisfaction at the transformation of the cabin. With Dolly and Al generously offering to chaperone, they and Garrett had helped her with final preparations for her family's arrival tomorrow.

A brightly lit evergreen—straight from the

local landscape nursery—now stood in a corner near the front window. She would let the kids decorate it when they arrived, just as she and her sisters used to do. Swags of greenery wrapped around support posts, and the nativity set—sans baby Jesus—stretched across the console table against the wall where it would be less likely to be knocked off by younger members of the family. Battery-lit candles flickered in the windows and on the mantel above a crackling fire, and the air held the subtle scent of pine and burning oak.

Garrett pulled out a chair for her at the big dining table. "Looks like something out of a magazine, doesn't it, Jodi?"

"Thanks to all of you."

"Your grandma would be so pleased with what you're doing for your nieces and nephew." Al reached out for Jodi's hand on one side and that of his wife on the other, preparing for the prayer. He nodded pointedly at her to take Garrett's hand on her other side, so she self-consciously slipped hers into Garrett's big, warm one and bowed her head.

Did Al and Dolly sense any difference in their interactions? Catch the furtive glances, the quick smiles, the lingering looks?

"Father God," Al began, "we thank You for this special season of remembering the most amazing gift You've bestowed on mankind, Your son,

Jesus Christ. We thank You that on that day in history, hope was given birth, a bridge so generously established between You and your prone-to-wander creation. We are, indeed, a people blessed. Thank You for this food and our time together this evening. In Your son's name, amen."

Garrett gently squeezed her hand as amens echoed around the table.

"Looks like you're ready to welcome your family. Around lunchtime you said?" Dolly opened a tall metal tin and pulled out a packet of saltines.

"Yes, they'll be driving up in the morning. Today's fresh snow should please the kids, but I think the roads should be mostly clear by tomorrow. I'm not sure, though, if anyone is really ready to open the doors to Henry."

"He's the four-year-old?"

"Lovable and huggable." She tucked her napkin across her lap. "But sometimes a real handful. He keeps Ronda on her toes every minute of the day just to prevent him from doing himself permanent injury. Right from the beginning he was one of those kids who refused to stay in his crib, always climbing up and out when no one was looking."

Dolly crushed a cracker into her soup as she slid an amused look in Garrett's direction. "Reminds me of someone I used to know."

"Hey, what can I say?" Garrett shrugged, not

looking the least bit repentant. "Henry sounds like my kind of guy. Some of us are born to adventure."

Like river-running—and a dangerous missions field?

She'd always loved sports. The outdoors. But she'd never been much of a risk taker—unless egged on by Garrett. They weren't to the point of discussing anything that smacked of a possible permanent union. But if things worked out between them, would he expect her to accompany him to the Middle East? Could the fledgling renewal of her faith lead her in that direction? Given a choice, she didn't even want to relocate overseas with her current job. But if that's where this relationship led, well, she'd support Garrett in his calling any way she could. She just needed to trust God would work things out as was best for both of them.

"If you and Henry are so simpatico," Jodi said, leveling a teasing look at Garrett, "I'm sure my sister would be happy to put you in charge of the little guy while he's here. She says she and her hubby feel God's given them a ministry to singles who think they want to be married and start a family. By the time they and Henry depart, singlehood is much more palatable."

Dolly cringed. "Oh, my."

A grinning Garrett reached for his spoon. "Bring him on."

The dinnertime conversation ebbed and flowed comfortably, and laughter often erupted. Al and Dolly appeared to feel perfectly at ease with her and Garrett. Of course, they'd known both of them since the two friends were little, and they'd housed Garrett this past year. No wonder she felt so comfortable, almost as if among family.

Not surprisingly, a twinge of disappointment burst her contented little bubble when Al inquired how the Christmas project was going. Due to all the preparations for her family's arrival and the fun flirtation with Garrett taking center stage, with the exception of a visit to Kimmy she'd let the project slide to the back burner of her mind. But with delivery only a few days away, she had limited time to pull it all together.

"Now, don't badger the girl." Dolly gave her husband a chastising look.

"I'm not badgering. Just showing interest."

And he probably was. But what about others who remembered the volume of donations in past years? Even though she'd been a part of the project barely over a week, would blame for a comparatively skimpy number of gifts be placed at her doorstep?

Would that, in turn, reflect poorly on Garrett? He already felt there were those in the congregation who believed he fell short of their expectations. Even though he didn't think fondly of the project, Randall Moppert, for one, would no doubt gleefully add this poor holiday showing to his growing list of pastoral shortcomings.

"The project's coming along," Jodi said lightly, then bit into one of Dolly's molasses cookies.

"We still have a few days left," Garrett encouraged. "Someone I know, who has overseen a lot of projects in the past, recently told me that you often hit a plateau on these kinds of things. Then suddenly it all falls into place."

Al nodded thoughtfully. "That so?"

"Makes sense to me." Dolly helped herself to a cookie. "You know, the old saying that it's always darkest before the dawn."

"True." Al broke his own cookie in quarters and popped a piece of it in his mouth.

Jodi cast Garrett a grateful look, and he winked.

Her face warmed. "Now that things are pretty much ready for my family and they won't arrive until midday tomorrow, I'll have time to make more phone calls. I'm thinking, too, that my time might be well spent making personal visits to businesses around town."

Al clapped his hands together. "Now you're talking, gal. Get right in their faces."

"It might not hurt." Dolly dusted the cookie crumbs from her fingers onto her plate. "It might be harder for someone to say no if you're standing there looking right at them."

Al placed his forearms on the table and leaned in Jodi's direction. "It's my guess that if you bat those big brown eyes of yours at them, you'll double your donations."

Dolly poked her husband's arm, but Al waved her off, turning his attention to Garrett. "Don't ya think so, Pastor McCrae?"

Garrett's eyes locked with hers as he placed his napkin on the table, a smile twitching at his lips. "I wouldn't be the least bit surprised, Al."

Al slapped the tabletop. "See? What did I tell you?"

"Now you two stop your teasin'." Dolly rose to clear away her and Al's plates. "You're making our poor Jodi blush."

"Just makes her all the prettier, right, Garrett?" The look Al shot in Garrett's direction was a little too knowing. Even if Dolly hadn't sensed a shift in Garrett's relationship with her, her husband had obviously caught on.

"You won't hear any arguments from me." Garrett, too, rose to gather both his and Jodi's plates, his eyes twinkling.

"Well, then," Al announced as he slid a mischievous look in Jodi's direction, "that eye-batting strategy sounds like a plan to me. One that I fully expect in the very near future to show... welcome results."

Chapter Thirteen

Sitting in a big wingback chair in front of the cabin's fireplace Wednesday evening, Garrett laughed as a freshly scrubbed and flannel-pajamaed Henry crawled into his lap, a picture book in hand.

Garrett had stopped by in the afternoon to join in building a snow fort—and just in time to rescue Jodi's intrepid nephew from where he'd climbed on the porch railing and shinnied up a support post to dangle precariously from the gutter. And that was only the first rescue of several before they'd all been called in for supper—and an evening of stringing popcorn, making paper-linked garlands and cutting out snowflakes for the tree.

In the two days since he and Jodi agreed to seek God's direction, they'd shared hours of fun and laughter, serious discussion, and catching each other up on their lives. In so many ways it was as if there had never been a dozen years between that first kiss and the one that had only recently been shared. They had so many values in common. Felt strongly about the bonds of family. Wanted to be used by God. Hour by hour, minute by minute, the connection between them deepened.

And yet…he still hadn't brought himself to tell her about the role he'd played in Drew's injuries, the instrumental turning point in his relationship with God.

Why was that? He trusted her. He did. She wouldn't reject him because of his past mistakes any more than he'd reject her because of hers. But he couldn't bear to see the disappointment in him that was certain to reflect in her beautiful eyes.

He looked over at Jodi on the sofa, occupied with a book and her two nieces. She glanced up. He winked, and she smiled back, relaxed, happy and the light in her eyes clearly communicating her contentment.

If only he could relax into that same God confidence she seemed to be growing into. But uncertainty nagged. Not about how he felt about Jodi, but about how they could work things out for a future together given his plans for the Middle East. No way would he take her there, even if she'd be willing to go.

And what about his sister and her two kids, who'd recently returned to town? They were shooting up so fast that if he blinked twice they'd be all grown up. He'd like to think their Uncle Garrett's presence these past few weeks had filled a need for a male role model if even in a small way. And then there was Grandma Jo—how many more years would she be around to enjoy? And what if Aunt Elaine's health took a turn for the worse?

He'd invested a lot of time and prayer in the church and community, as well. Would his labor continue to bear fruit after he was gone? Would someone else pick up where he left off, or would the ball get dropped and roll off into the shadows?

Henry, paging through the book, cuddled closer, and Garrett gave him a hug.

Those things hadn't troubled him until Jodi's return. Previously he'd been able to shut them out at their first nagging glimmer. But not now. Which didn't exactly make him a cheerful holiday elf deep down inside, although he was doing his best to put on a good front.

Today he'd relished watching Jodi with the kids. Although she claimed not to have much experience with children, no one let that fact form a barrier between them and their Aunt Jodi.

And he, despite laughing protests, had been dubbed Uncle Garrett. He had to admit he liked the sound of that, and it seemed to amuse Star and Ronda. Both had a good laugh at their sister's expense, too, when he admitted he had a turkey thawing at his place in case they wanted to put the kibosh on Jodi's plans for a catered Christmas dinner. They took him up on his offer immediately and, thankfully, Jodi hadn't yet gotten around to placing an order.

It was obvious they sensed something between him and Jodi that they hadn't expected to see when they'd arrived. Something of which, from all appearances, they wholeheartedly approved. If he wasn't mistaken, Al and Dolly had also caught on to the shift between him and Jodi and were pleased.

Lord, it would be so easy to let myself love her. To love her family. But I know that may be something on down the road. Not for now.

Until Jodi had come back into his life, he'd assumed he'd be overseas for the long haul. But now his focus had shifted. More and more he found his thoughts drifting to Jodi. To his family. To the souls in Hunter Ridge. Now that he'd spoken up about his mission plans and admitted to an interest in Jodi, well, it didn't seem as if reconciling the two directions was as easily resolved as he'd first led himself to believe.

"*Read*, Uncle Garrett." Henry firmly patted the open book.

Garrett glanced again at Jodi, Bethany and Savannah cuddled on either side of her. But the warming of his heart only somewhat overrode the uncertainties dwelling there. Although he'd boldly talked of God's timing, of waiting for His leading, he'd need to make a decision soon about if—and how—he could work Jodi into his life. Although the thought of losing her left an ache in his heart, he didn't want to lead her on.

Would God have brought her back into his life only to ask him to give her up?

She'd had it rough since leaving Hunter Ridge. Thankfully, he'd been present tonight at dinner when Ronda announced her latest pregnancy, and he was able to unobtrusively slip his hand around Jodi's and give it a squeeze. While she'd earlier claimed to be struggling in her faith, though, he sensed a growing peacefulness in her these past few days. The peacefulness of this holy season that he longed to share.

He gave himself a mental shake and wrapped his arms more tightly around Henry. Then, opening the colorfully illustrated book to the first page, he cleared his throat and started reading aloud.

With the sun attempting to peep between layers of clouds, Jodi pulled into the church parking lot Thursday morning, hoping to use plans to prepare a gift-wrapping center for donations as an excuse to pop in and say hello to Garrett before paying visits to business owners. In addition to a boatload of wrapping paper, tape, ribbon and bows, with Garrett assuring her that he and Sofia had never taken an interest in each other, she'd even brought cookies just as Sofia had been known to do.

Not that she'd baked them herself.

Star had supplemented a college scholarship by working at a grocery store's bakery, and her acquired skills were out of this world. Jodi didn't think Garrett would mind that she hadn't assisted in their preparation—except to lick a spoon.

Her spirits rose at the prospect of making the delivery and a chance to visit with him this morning. She'd sensed that something was troubling him, that he wasn't sharing the same hopeful feelings of the holiday that she'd been flooded with the past few days. When he left last night, she'd stepped out on the porch to ask him if everything was all right. But he'd responded with a typical Garrett smile, reassuring her that it was merely a busy time of year and apologizing for being distracted.

Maybe that was all it was. Or maybe not.

Plastic wrap–covered cookie plate in hand, she'd just slammed the truck's door when she spied Drew's van in the parking lot and noticed him outside the fellowship hall. He struggled to hold the door open as he balanced a large cardboard box on his lap.

She was at his side in a flash. "Could you use some help?"

"Hey, there, Jodi! Great timing. The automatic door doesn't want to stay open long enough for me to get myself inside."

"Let me hold it." She stepped around his wheelchair to grasp the handle. "I'll mention to Dolly to get someone in to take a look at it."

"Thanks." He angled his motorized chair and slipped inside. When she entered, he spun the chair to face her, his eyes holding a speculative gleam as he spied the cookies. "You're looking pretty chipper this morning. Anything special going on in your life?"

Garrett. Garrett. Garrett.

But it was too premature to mention that to Drew. "There's a team coming to wrap presents for the Christmas project this afternoon. I'm here to get things set up, and that puts me in the holiday spirit."

He gave her a somewhat skeptical look, but didn't probe further. "So how's that going? Did you get the donations you'd hoped for?"

"Not as many as I'd like, but people are being as generous as they can."

He patted the side of the cardboard box. "Well, maybe this will help."

Touched that Drew would think to donate something to aid unwed mothers, she set the cookie plate on a nearby table, then stepped forward as he lifted the lid. She peered inside the box, filled with stuffed toys of every imaginable kind. Bears. Puppies. Kittens. Whales. Turtles.

"Ohhh, Drew! Thank you." She leaned over to give him a hug, then reached in to pull out a silky soft penguin and cuddled it close. "Where on earth did you find these?"

"As usual, I let my credit card do all the walking—online. These were delivered last night."

She placed the penguin back in the box and lifted out a zebra. "These are adorable. You are such a sweetheart."

"And speaking of sweethearts… I'm especially curious seeing those cookies over there. How's my old buddy treating you? I'd have to be blind not to notice there's something going on between the two of you since you came back."

Her face warmed as she focused her attention on the black-and-white-striped critter in her hands. Was it that obvious? "You know we're good friends."

"Tell me another one. Garrett's acting kind of secretive, too. So what's up?"

She couldn't tell a bold-faced lie. But she

was limited in what she could say. While hopes abounded, there wasn't anything concrete yet. They'd talked of being open to God's leading, but neither had uttered the word *love* or made any promises, although she knew, for her part anyway, that was the state of her own heart.

"I think…we're exploring how we feel about each other."

Drew raised a brow. "Exploring?"

"Prayerfully," she quickly added, "asking God to show us if He wants us to move beyond friends."

"I may be mistaken, but it appears to me it's already gone beyond that."

"We don't want to get ahead of ourselves— or God. There are a number of things yet to be worked through, some potential roadblocks, including Garrett's plans for the future."

Drew chuckled. "Garrett has plans for the future? You mean beyond the next five minutes?"

"Going into missions is a big step."

Drew raised his hand. "Whoa, whoa. Stop right there. Missions? Garrett has plans to be a missionary? Since when?"

A muscle in Jodi's stomach tightened. *Drew didn't know?*

Had she let something slip that Garrett didn't want shared with his longtime friend? Her mind raced frantically, recalling earlier conversations.

He'd said, when he told her of his plans, that he hadn't shared his intentions with many. But surely the ones he'd told would have included the minister in Canyon Springs and Drew, wouldn't they? Especially since Drew had such a heart for those in the Middle East. Garrett would want his support, his assistance, his prayers.

"He didn't—?"

"Tell me? You'd think he would have, wouldn't you? But this is the first I'm hearing of this." Drew's brows lowered and his jaw hardened, suddenly a formidable-looking man. "He wouldn't be planning on a destination in the Middle East, would he?"

Jodi stared at him as his gaze pierced into hers. She'd unintentionally stirred up a hornet's nest. "I shouldn't be discussing this. You need to talk to Garrett."

He slammed his fist on the arm of his wheelchair, startling her. "He is, isn't he? That's where he's going. Don't you get it? He's going to the very place I was headed before *this* happened."

He roughly motioned to his legs.

Now she understood his anger. Garrett was taking over his dream, doing something Drew long had a stake in, but his damaged body would no longer permit him to fulfill the requirements.

"I'm sure he didn't intend to hurt you. That's probably why he didn't say anything about his plans and his destination. He didn't want to make you feel bad that you couldn't go, too."

Drew shook his head. "No, no, no. Don't you get it? My feelings aren't hurt. But I *am* mad. He's doing this out of guilt."

"Guilt for what?"

"He somehow has it all messed up in his mind that he can somehow pay God—and me—back for the misguided responsibility he's assuming for my accident."

Jodi tensed. Garrett was involved in Drew's accident?

"He blames himself because we were on a rafting trip on the Colorado. One he'd badgered me to go on before I headed back out on another missions trip. We'd hiked into a side canyon early one evening to do some swimming. Got clowning around just like we often did. Thinking to evade Garrett, I… I dived into the water—and didn't clear a slab of stone lurking under the surface."

With a soft gasp, she pressed her fingers momentarily to her lips. "Oh, Drew."

"He dived in and kept me from drowning. Got me air vacced out of there to Flagstaff. But he's had a hard time letting go of the possibility that moving me, pulling me out, is what really caused the injury."

"But if he hadn't taken action, you'd—"

"Be dead. Guaranteed. But he still feels responsible since he was one of the crew. He said he'd never have allowed any of the other guests on the trip to do what we were doing."

"So you think he's going to the Middle East…"

"Because *I* can't. I'm certain of it." Drew smacked the palm of his hand on the arm of his wheelchair. "God used the accident to get his attention. But in all these five years, I had no idea he harbored an intent to do missions work in the Middle East. Never." Drew fisted his fingers. "And when I get my hands around his throat—"

"But you don't know what God—"

"This is God's doing? We both know Garrett can hands-down physically deal with the rigors of a commitment like that. But what I can't see is that his heart is in it." Drew's frown deepened. "I lived and breathed my devotion to the people of that part of the world. I studied the languages, the cultures, the political and religious and economic issues. I openly immersed myself in prayer for that region. Still do. But Garrett's kept his intent a secret from everyone. Doesn't that strike you as odd?"

"Maybe he knew he'd get pushback from you. From others."

"I'm not buying that it's his calling. In the twelve short months that he's been back in Hunter Ridge, he's been instrumental in reviving this church. In drawing local and regional churches together to cooperate for God's goal of meeting spiritual and physical needs. You've only been here a short time, but that's got to be apparent to you, too. This is where his gifts lie. His calling. How can he not see that?"

In spite of his protests that some in the church would be happy to see him go, Garrett seemed ideally suited to the ministry he'd been given here. From all evidence, he was making a difference. Who was to say, though, that God might not call him elsewhere? But Drew's concerns were also legitimate. Had Garrett's intended destination been anywhere but the Middle East...

Drew grasped Jodi's arm. "If he thinks he can slip out of town without looking me square in the eye and telling me he's not doing this out of a guilty conscience, he's got another think coming."

With that, Drew released her and spun his wheelchair around, smacked his hands against the bar on the exit door and pushed his way out of the building.

Shaken, Jodi stared after him until the door slammed closed. Why had Garrett never shared any of this about the accident with her? She'd poured out her heart to him regarding her own regrets. Had allowed him to hold her, comfort her. Yet he'd harbored a deep wound of his own, never allowing her the opportunity to reciprocate.

Hurt, her gaze swept the open space where

not many days ago they'd inventoried the donations—then beyond to the hallway that led to his office. She had to get the wrapping supplies brought in and the workstations set up. If she hurried, though, there would be time enough to have a word with him before she met the others at lunch. She needed to explain to him in person how she'd inadvertently brought his plans to the attention of Drew.

Could Garrett's friend be right? Was he doing this for all the wrong reasons? And how might questioning his motives impact their newly fledged relationship?

Chapter Fourteen

"Get off my case, Drew."

Irritation rising, Garrett held the cell phone to his ear as he paced the living room floor of the Lovells' house, grateful that the older couple had gone to see friends that morning and he'd had the place to himself to work on his Christmas Eve message.

"You've been holding out on me, buddy. Until Jodi let it slip, I had no idea you intended to set sail for the same destination I'd mapped out."

Jodi had betrayed his confidence?

"So you think," Drew continued, his tone harsh, "that you can make up for what happened that day on the river?"

"Nothing will ever make up for that day on the river. Don't talk crazy."

"I don't think it's me talking crazy here. Why'd

you keep this a secret? Is it a done deal? You've signed on the dotted line?"

"Not yet, but I will. Soon." He'd originally applied right out of college and been turned down, but now he had a year's worth of ministry experience under his belt and, hopefully, would be receiving a strong enough recommendation from church leadership to get him in the door.

Drew's voice raised a notch. "This is nuts. You've never said a peep about being into foreign missions, let alone something like the Middle East."

"You don't think I can handle it?" He'd done his best to stay in top shape since leaving the demands of river rafting.

"The physical rigors, you mean? That's not the issue here. I'm talking about following what God's put in your heart. Honing what He's gifted you to do."

Garrett ran his hand roughly through his hair. "I may not have made a public service announcement at the time, but this dream has long been in my heart. It's what pulled me from the river and into Bible college."

"Your dream—or mine? You used to tell me I was out of my mind to trek all over the globe, risking my neck to tell people about Jesus who'd just as soon kill me as look at me. You said I had a death wish, remember?"

"Think back, Drew. That was before God recruited me to His team."

"Which happened, I will remind you, after the river incident."

"I wish you and everyone else would stop calling that an incident. It makes it sound as if you'd done nothing more than stubbed your toe."

Garrett heard his friend draw a labored breath and braced himself for another verbal assault. But it didn't come. Instead, Drew's tone quieted.

"We've been friends a long time, Garrett."

"Yeah, we have."

"As a friend, as one who walks by your side on God's path, I'm asking you to step back and reevaluate this."

"Listen, Drew—"

"No, *you* listen. I don't like being wheelchair-bound. I don't like being kept off the mission fields while they are ripe for harvest. But don't you think if God had wanted me back out there, that He could have prevented what happened from happening? That He could have had me dive in just a few inches from that submerged rock? Don't you think God's big enough, in control enough, that He could have done that?"

Garrett gripped the phone more tightly. "You're not saying God *made* this happen, are you? That He would—"

"No! But things happen. Accidents. Our souls

are housed in a temporary, sometimes-fragile physical home that often takes a beating. I pray for God's healing daily, but I've accepted where I am. Accepted that God can still use me for a good purpose. But *you've* let my situation eat at you for the past five years and have somehow gotten things all twisted up in your mind."

Garrett grimaced. "Thanks for the vote of confidence."

"You know what I mean. You're so gifted, so God-empowered for a ministry like the one you're growing at Christ's Church. You're reaching people I could never have reached while off in the Middle East—people I'm not even reaching now that I'm right back here in our hometown. But *you* are."

At the sound of a slamming car door, Garrett's attention was drawn to the window. Rio's truck out by the curb. Which meant… A moment later the doorbell rang.

"I've got to go, Drew. Someone's at the door."

"You don't owe me or God a single thing, bud. Promise me you'll rethink this. Pray about it."

"Look, I've got to go."

"Right." For a moment he thought Drew would continue, but he abruptly disconnected.

Garrett stuffed his cell phone back in his pocket. Jodi was here, and with his SUV sitting in the gravel area next to the driveway, he couldn't pretend not to be home.

He hurt not only from Drew's verbal thrashing, but from the fact that Jodi had shared his plans with his friend. Had she done it intentionally? Hoping Drew would try to dissuade him from following through? No, he refused to believe that.

Lord, please let me respond to her as a man of God should.

He pulled the door open to face Jodi, her gaze faltering as she offered a smile and held out a plate of cookies. A peace offering?

"Hey, Garrett."

"Hey."

"Have a minute? Marisela was at the church office and said you were working from home. There's something I need to talk to you about."

He held open the storm door, and she slipped in past him, out of the cold, to set the cookies on a nearby table.

"I think I made a mistake." She looked at him uncertainly. "I didn't know you hadn't told one of your best friends about your missions plans. And I didn't know your destination had been *his* plan before the accident. He wasn't happy, so I think you'll be hearing from him."

"Already have."

She winced. "I'm sorry. I tried to get here as fast as I could to tell you, but I had to—"

"It's okay. He was bound to find out sooner or later."

"It wasn't my intention to say something I shouldn't have. But in some ways, it helps to understand things better."

"Like what?"

"Why you're driven to an especially dangerous type of missions work." She hesitated, her eyes searching his. "Drew believes you're trying to make up to him—and God—the fact that he can no longer actively participate in field work."

"He told you about the part I played in his injuries, did he?" He knew she'd eventually find out, he just didn't think the time would come so soon. "I'm sorry, Jodi. You should have heard it from me."

"I don't fault you for that. I know it must be hard to talk about. But please don't be mad at Drew for telling me. He thinks the world of you and is concerned that you're giving up your position in Hunter Ridge. Both of us can see what an amazing difference you're making in this town."

"You forget, Jodi, there is no position to give up. I haven't been offered a contract extension."

She grimaced. "I still don't understand that, but we believe God's gifted you in so many ways for small-town ministry. I'm sure other churches in little towns are looking for someone just like you."

"Gifted for small-town ministry, but not to touch the lives of those elsewhere?"

"That's not what we're saying. It's just that—"

"It's not about where I'm most gifted, is it?" he said gently, an ache forming in his heart. He didn't like where this conversation might be leading. Surely God wouldn't...

Jodi had lost a love on the mission field. It was only natural she'd hesitate to face the possibility of reliving something like that again. He should have recognized that earlier. They'd talked tentatively of a future together. No promises. No timelines. Yet clearly moving in that direction. But he wasn't being fair to her. "You don't want me to go, do you?"

"I— It's not that I don't want you to go if that's where God is leading you. It's that I want you to be sure. Drew wants you to be sure."

"I'm certain, Jodi. God put this on my heart years ago when He called me away from a job I loved. He gave me a purpose. His purpose."

"Or a means to pay Him back because you took one of His most valuable players out of the game?" He flinched inwardly, and apparently startled by her own words, Jodi reached out to grasp his arm. "I'm sorry, Garrett. I shouldn't have said it like that."

God, please don't take this where I think you're

taking it. Don't ask me to— "I know you mean well, Jode, but—"

"You and I've been friends since we were kids, and in these weeks since I came back to town, I believe those bonds have greatly strengthened." Her grip tightened on his arm, her eyes pleading just as his heart was now pleading before God. "We know each other well, maybe as well or better than anyone else knows us."

Before he could open his mouth to respond, she rushed on. "I can't pretend that I understand what you feel is the direction that God is asking you to go. But I wouldn't be a true friend if I didn't point out that this direction rings of taking up Drew's dream—and not God's will."

He drew a breath, the ache inside growing heavier. *Jodi, his sweet Jodi.* The woman he'd only days ago come to believe might be the choice of God's heart for him, doubted him. Doubted he'd heard from God.

Amid the heady feelings he and Jodi had cautiously expressed to each other, hadn't doubts as to how things could work out still lingered on his part? Had God been trying to tell him that despite being head over heels for Jodi, that's not the direction He wanted them to go? Had he, in his growing love, ventured too far from God's intended purpose for his life when he'd allowed himself to reconnect with her?

She didn't support him, *couldn't* support him in this venture. And it was wrong of him to ask her to. To expect her to put her life on hold while he invested his in a dangerous corner of the world. To force her to live in fear of something happening to him just as had happened to her Anton.

But could he bring himself to sacrifice everything that he'd hoped and prayed for between the two of them? As much as he hated it, as much as it felt as if the chest that housed his heart was cracking, splintering, he had to.

For Jodi's sake.

He reached for her hands, grateful that his weren't shaking. "I believe…we've come to a crossroads."

"What do you mean?"
Please, please, not what I think he means.

She tightened her grip on his hands, attempting to draw from them a strength she knew she didn't possess. Not if, from the sorrowful look in his eyes, he was about to say what she feared he was preparing to say.

"We've been friends a long time, Jodi. Good friends." His thumbs gently stroked the backs of her hands. "But as much as we might have recently hoped for something more, I'm now—very sadly—recognizing that friendship is all God wants us to share."

Please, no.

Heart crumbling, she stared into Garrett's unwavering gaze as she tried to form a response. But no words came. In her effort to help him, she'd pushed him too far. Right out of her life.

Although his eyes remained bleak, he offered a tentative smile. "Friendship isn't a bad thing, Jode. Not an inferior thing, as some might believe. True friendships, like ours, stand the test of time. Far too many romantic ones often falter and fail."

She ducked her head, not wanting him to see the pricking tears.

"I know this is catching you off guard. Believe me, it's caught me off guard, too. I'd hoped—" He glanced away, then took a slow breath.

"Is it because I told Drew about your plans? Because I—"

"No, Jodi. It's not anything you did or didn't do. It's about us. About listening to God. Being willing to obey when He shows us where to go. Only a few days ago, we agreed to that, remember? To put our trust in Him? But I have to admit, I didn't expect an answer—*this* answer—to come so swiftly."

She lifted her head. "We can't...go in the same direction?"

He gave her hands a gentle squeeze as he looked down at her, his eyes filled with compassion. "I think you know the answer to that. You understand, don't you, where I'm coming from?"

She swallowed. And nodded. She knew what he was saying. But understand?

I will not cry.

Gently pulling her hands away from his, she turned away, afraid he'd see the trembling of her lower lip. "I'd better get going."

He caught her arm, his eyes alarmed. "Talk to me, Jodi. Don't rush off. I didn't mean for you to—"

"I'm not rushing off, but if I don't go now, I'll be late." She paused to catch her breath in an effort to keep her voice from cracking. "I'm treating the project volunteers to lunch. Then we're having a gift-wrapping party."

As if she were in the mood for that now? *Please, Lord, don't let him invite himself along.*

"It sounds like you have a busy afternoon planned." He almost sounded hurt that she had plans that didn't include him. But did he honestly think she'd want to hang out with him after what he'd just said?

With ice-cold fingers, she secured her scarf around her neck and turned to the door.

"If you want to, Jodi, we can talk about this more later." He looked at her uncertainly, as if it finally dawned on him that something he'd obviously been giving considerable thought had come as a complete surprise to her. "I *will* be seeing you around, right? Before you leave town?"

She forced what she trusted would pass as a genuine smile. A good old tomboy-Jodi version as she fisted her hand and popped him lightly on the shoulder as she would have done when teasing him as a twelve-year-old. "Sure."

Looking somewhat bewildered, he held the door open for her. She stepped outside to jog across the snowy yard with what she hoped looked like a carefree lope. But by the time she reached the truck, her hands were shaking so badly she could barely insert the key into the ignition. Pressing her lips tightly together, still holding back tears as she pulled away, she managed a cheery wave to where he stood watching from the doorway.

She didn't drive immediately to the Log Cabin Café to meet her friends. Although she'd used it as an excuse to escape Garrett, she had a little time to spare. With her family at the cabin, she couldn't go there, so she quickly found herself on a Forest Service road. Not far enough in to get her in any kind of trouble, but out of sight of the main road.

And there she parked and turned off the ignition.

She didn't dare allow herself to cry, or the volunteers meeting her for lunch would pick up on it. While she might be able to pass it off as a sentimental day with memories of her grandparents, that would be a lie.

Just like the lie she'd told Garrett—or rather, what Garrett assumed from her nod of agreement when he asked if she understood where he was coming from.

Oh, yes, she understood. Too clearly. Although only days ago he'd claimed otherwise—and that kiss, too, testified otherwise—he still couldn't get beyond his childhood memories of her. Jodi his pal. His buddy. His tomboy partner in crime.

She'd spoken to him bluntly about his mission plans—as friend to friend. Not lover to lover. That had been her downfall.

For the second time in her life, she'd allowed Garrett McCrae to raise her romantic hopes to crazy, dreamed-of heights, only to drop her crashing to the ground as he walked away, his own heart unscathed.

"How could I have let this happen again, Lord?" She stared up into the gray heavens, blinking hard to hold back the tears. "And how could *You* have let this happen to me?"

The accusation hung in the chilly air, the silence of the forest surrounding her pressing in close. Then she humbly bowed her head and fell into her Heavenly Father's comforting arms.

Chapter Fifteen

"We haven't seen you in a while." Grandma Jo placed her hands on her trousers-clad hips, looking Garrett over with a critical eye as he walked in the entryway door to his folks' cabin that evening.

He'd hoped that dinner with his parents, sister and her kids might get his mind off his last encounter with Jodi. It didn't take any genius to figure out he'd upset her. And when she hurt, he hurt. This isn't how either of them anticipated things would turn out between them. But given a little time, she'd see the wisdom in his decision, wouldn't she? See that he'd made it for her. Not because he didn't care, but because...he loved her.

An evening with his family was just what the doctor ordered. But he hadn't counted on Grandma Jo being here, too.

Garrett pulled off his jacket and hung it on

a wall peg next to the others. "It's a busy time of year."

"And from what I'm hearing, you're even busier renewing your friendship with Jodi Thorpe."

Friendship. That's all. He'd made sure of that. But where was the promised peace that was to come with making a right decision? "What is it you're hearing?"

"A little Travis bird mentioned seeing the two of you at dinner one night." A twinkle lit her eyes. "And you wouldn't believe the number of people who've reported that they've seen your SUV over at the cabin since she returned."

Little towns. A weariness settled into his heart.

"Don't worry, Grandma—we're always chaperoned." Except for the short interlude that morning at the Lovells' house. Could that land him in hot water? "Either Dolly or Jodi's sisters or somebody else I've dragged along."

"I'm not worried. Not about that, anyway."

It wasn't like Grandma Jo, usually a straight shooter, to beat around the bush. No way, though, could it have gotten around town already that he wouldn't be here much longer. Drew would respect his privacy even if he didn't agree with him. Jodi wouldn't have said anything to anyone, either—at least he didn't think she would.

"But I take it you *are* worried about something having to do with me?"

"*Concerned* might be a better word. Have you heard from church leadership regarding your future at Christ's Church?"

He couldn't keep hiding his plans from Grandma much longer. Pretty soon everyone in town would know, and she shouldn't be the last. "No, I haven't."

"I was under the impression—" She abruptly cut herself off.

"That they'd have the courtesy to let me know by now that my contract won't be renewed? I came into this interim position a year ago knowing it wasn't permanent, that it was merely a refueling stop between college and what I really planned to do."

Her brows raised slightly. "You've made other plans?"

"I walked into this job with other plans. If all works out, not long after the first of the year I hope to be in language and culture training. And eventually in foreign missions."

She stared at him. "Where?"

"Middle East. Wherever I'm needed to meet the practical and spiritual needs of war torn countries. Wherever God sends me."

"Why there?" Her gaze was as sharp as her words. "That's where Drew intended to go, isn't it?"

"God handed off the baton."

"Are you certain, Garrett?"

"Grandma, I know you've wanted me to minister here in Hunter Ridge ever since I told you I'd decided to go to Bible college. But that's not where my focus is. It's not where it's ever been."

"Do your parents know?"

"Not yet. I'm sorry I didn't tell you sooner. I felt it was better kept to myself until my year here was over."

Or had he been hoping God would change His mind?

She frowned. "What does Jodi think of this? Is she going to let you carry her off with you into those dangerous regions?"

"Jodi and I are friends. Nothing more. I hadn't seen or spoken to her in twelve years. Sure, we were best buds as kids, but people grow up. Change. She's here until just after Christmas, and I won't be here much longer than that."

For the first time in his remembrance since Grandpa had passed away, Grandma Jo looked lost. "I don't know what to think of all this."

"Be happy for me, Grandma. And pray for my safety and that I'll be a blessing wherever one is needed most. That's all I ask."

She nodded, but her gaze remained troubled. Which did nothing, as he slipped past her in search of the rest of his family, to usher in that peace he'd been praying for.

* * *

"It was totally amazing what we accomplished this afternoon," Jodi called to her sisters as she removed her boots and peeled out of her jacket. She hung the latter on a peg, then joined her siblings in the kitchen where she further boosted a happy lilt to her voice that she didn't feel. "I don't think I've ever seen that many wrapped and be-ribboned packages in one place in my whole life. All neatly labeled for easy identification and distribution. It was so much fun."

But she'd hoped for more donations and hadn't had time to make many of the face-to-face visits that Al was certain would bring more rolling in. She feared, when hearing the other women describe the carloads of presents delivered in the past, that she'd fallen far short of Melody's legacy.

And Garrett's expectations.

As the children's chatter carried from the living room area, Star pulled a stack of bowls from one of the cabinets and handed them to her. "You're delivering tomorrow, right?"

"Right. Most of it will be taken to the church in Canyon Springs, where volunteers will group the packages for the regional pregnancy centers and those with four-wheel drives will see that gifts get out even to the more remote areas. Like the reservation. I delivered a few packages on my way back here, too." She couldn't resist stopping by to see Kimmy. "That's why I'm running late. Thanks for holding supper for me. It smells delicious."

Tonight's treat was beanless beef chili, the kind served on top of a fluffy bed of rice and finished off with a dollop of sour cream and grated cheddar.

"Is Garrett joining us?" Ronda rummaged in the silverware drawer, searching for enough spoons. "He used to love Grandma's chili."

A knot tightened in Jodi's stomach as she paused in placing the bowls around the table. "Actually…he has things to take care of this evening. Christmas is a busy time for him."

"A preacher's work is never done, I guess. At least we can put some aside in the freezer and give it to him the next time he pops in."

She didn't have the heart to tell her sister he wouldn't be popping in. Ever.

A cheery ringtone alerted her that she had an incoming call, and reaching into the pocket of her knit vest, she retrieved it. Melody Lenter, at long last. With the family noisily congregating in the main room, she quickly moved into the hallway near the bedrooms for privacy.

A tingle of apprehension touched the back of her neck. Would the other woman be disappointed when she learned donations weren't up to that of past years? So many people said they'd already donated. And although she'd explained that apparently emergency needs had come up that required raiding the intended Christmas gifts, some were sincerely unable to contribute further.

She caught the call on its final ring. "Melody! We meet at last."

"I'm so sorry, Jodi." A lilting Southern drawl carried through the ear piece. "I kept thinkin' I'd have me some time to get back to you, but Daddy's been in and out of the hospital. And now his oldest sister and her husband have come down with the flu and I'm running back and forth between the two households, trying to keep everybody fed and watered. It's just one thing after another."

"Sounds exhausting."

"When you talk to our good pastor, please let him know I'll do my best to be back right after the first of the year. No promises. But after the holidays my sister will be in town and can spell me for a while." Melody paused to draw a breath. "So how are things going with the Christmas project? Fun, isn't it, honey?"

"It has been." She could be honest about that. For the most part, anyway. After she'd better come to terms with past issues that had held her hostage for way too long, she'd actually enjoyed it.

"Have y'all made the deliveries? Christmas is only a few days away."

"We're teaming up with Canyon Springs Christian to get that taken care of tomorrow."

"Perfect. It sounds as if everything's under control."

"I hope you won't be too disappointed with the outcome of leaving the project in the hands of a stranger. I understand you've faithfully overseen it for quite a few years."

"Now, why would I be disappointed? I trust Garrett to have found someone capable of handling it. I'm sure you've done a fine job."

"I can't help but wish, though, that we could have filled the storeroom to overflowing."

"That shouldn't have been *too* hard to do. It was three-quarters full already."

Obviously, the stress of being a full-time caregiver had rattled the woman's memory. "When Garrett first showed me the storeroom, it was all but empty."

Jody cringed as the woman laughed, not taking her revelation seriously.

"You must have looked in the wrong storage room."

"Little snowman on the door?"

Melody gasped.

"There was a single package of disposable diapers, to be exact," Jodi added.

"No way. No way." She was obviously in denial. "There were stacks of those. And maternity and baby clothes. Cases of baby wipes and formula, bottles, you name it. It was like a baby warehouse."

"None of that."

"Someone must have broken in and—" The woman went abruptly silent. Had she fainted from shock?

"Melody?"

Then came a giggle. A giggle that immediately erupted into a full-fledged belly laugh. Had the poor woman lost her mind?

"Melody?"

"Oh my goodness." The words came between raspy gasps. Half laugh, half wheezing for air. "Oh, my. Oh, my. Oh, my."

"Are you okay?"

"The exterminator." She broke out in laughter again.

She'd gone off the deep end. Garrett had mentioned she could sometimes be a bit flighty, but hadn't mentioned anything to this extreme.

"You've lost me, Melody." She didn't want to push her, but surely something more lucid would come forth if she was encouraged to explain.

"The exterminator. The bug guy, honey." Melody laughed again. "He was scheduled for his quarterly visit and no way did I want him prowling around squirting his little chemicals in the nooks and crannies of that storeroom. They claim that stuff is harmless, but I didn't want to risk pregnant mamas or little ones being exposed to anything dangerous. So the weekend before he was to come, Ralph and I—Ralph's my husband—hauled all the donations over to our house."

"Are you saying there are *more* gifts somewhere?"

"Tons, honey, tons. In our guest room. The day after we moved them out of the church, I got the call about Daddy. So Ralph and I took off. I didn't give it a second thought that we'd temporarily moved everything off the premises. I remembered to call Garrett and tell him we were leaving town, but that's about it." She gave another laugh. "Poor Pastor McCrae, I bet he just about fell through the floor when he opened that door to an empty room."

"Close to it."

"Well, honey, you just apologize to him for me. And if you knock on Sissy Taylor's door, my neighbor to the north, she can lend you my house key and get you right in there. Will that give you time to wrap everything and make deliveries?"

Did she have any choice? But her relief at being able to meet everyone's expectations was so immense she wouldn't have cared if she personally had to stay up all night long and wrap every single item all by herself.

"It's doable."

"I'm so glad we could finally connect tonight." Melody giggled again. "And that you reminded me of what I'd done with all those donations I've been collecting since early summer."

"Garrett remembered the storeroom being fuller a few months ago, but thought there had been some maternity-related emergencies."

"I dipped into it a time or two. But not in a major way." A happy sigh carried over the phone. "Well, all's well that ends well, right? I've got to run. Hear Daddy calling for me. But honey, I do wish you the best of Christmases. And you give our favorite pastor a big holiday hug from me, will you?"

"I—"

"Take care now."

Jodi remained standing in the hallway for a long moment, stunned at this unexpected turn of events. Then, like Melody, she couldn't help but laugh as she again joined her sisters in the kitchen, her mind overcome with wonder. "Wow."

"Wow, what?" Star demanded.

"From that smile on your face—" Ronda cut her a mischievous look as she stirred the chili "—I'm guessing that was a call from Garrett."

Jodi's high spirits faltered, but she made a

funny face at her sister. "Nooo. Remember how I said donations for the Christmas project weren't up to previous years? How I felt I'd let everyone down? Well, that was Melody, who has headed up the project for years. And guess what?"

Ronda placed her hands on her hips. "I'm not going to guess, Jodi. Just tell us."

"She'd forgotten that before she made an emergency trip out of town that she'd taken a storage space full of donations to her house for safekeeping"

Both sisters squealed.

"This is fantastic." Ronda's face almost glowed, then her eyes widened with alarm. "Are they already wrapped or will you have to do that before making deliveries tomorrow?"

"Unwrapped." But she didn't care. "I'll make some phone calls—get Melody's house key and round up volunteers to come in early to transfer the gifts to the church."

"Let us know if there's anything we can do to help."

Thank you, thank you, Lord. After supper she'd call around for a wrapping crew and a few more cars and drivers. It was a last-minute job she wouldn't mind doing in the least, and she imagined the others would be happy to pitch in again, too. Garrett would be delighted.

At the thought of Garrett, a queasy feeling rolled over in her stomach. Should she call him, too, and let him in on the good news?

Chapter Sixteen

"Do you have time for a quick chat, Pastor McCrae?"

From where he sat at his desk early Friday morning, typing up notes for Sunday's Christmas message, Garrett looked up at church board members Bert Palmer and Julian Gonzales standing in his open office doorway.

He'd been expecting this "chat" for weeks. While it wouldn't be comfortable hearing them deliver the expected message, at least he'd had other plans all along.

"Sure, come on in." Garrett stood, motioning them to the seating area. Julian closed the door to give them privacy, and the three settled into the wingback chairs.

"Hard to believe, isn't it?" Julian ventured. "A whole year has gone by since you signed on to pastor Christ's Church. You've probably been wondering why we haven't come to see you sooner. You know, about your future here."

"I admit I thought I might hear from you earlier."

"We apologize for that," Julian continued as the two board members exchanged a glance. "It wasn't our intention to leave you hanging. But there have been issues involved that required input and resolution."

"Understandable." They probably had members lined up out the door, eager to share lamentations on the performance of their interim pastor. A few of the complainants might even have been his own extended family members. Hadn't Luke been known to scold him for not following protocol?

"But before you continue, though—" Garrett wanted to smooth the path for the pair he'd come to highly respect this past year. "I'd like to say that working with you and the other church members has been an experience that I'm deeply thankful for. It's been a growing time. A stretching time. A time of blessing. I don't regret having taken on this filler role until you could find a permanent replacement."

The men exchanged glances again.

"Fire away, then, gentlemen. And don't hold anything back. I can take my lumps like a man."

Bert frowned. "Lumps?"

"I mean, you don't have to sugarcoat anything. I'm well aware of my shortcomings and the areas in which I still need to grow. I know that at times I haven't met expectations and have probably let you down."

Julian shifted in his chair. "I can't say we agree with your self-evaluation, Garrett. At least not the way you've worded it. Quite frankly, we've been delighted that you *haven't* met our original expectations."

"Or rather, our concerns," Bert clarified. "As you probably guessed, we had our doubts when your grandma approached us about you after yet another pastor pulled out to leave us sitting high and dry. You'd left behind a pretty wild legacy when you headed out of town after high school. And after that, Drew Everton's accident."

Bert looked uncomfortable at having to bring that up.

"Again, I fully understand." At least he hadn't disappointed them entirely. "And in spite of your reservations, thank you for the opportunity you've given me to take part in ministering to my hometown."

Julian grinned. "Sounds to me, then, that you're willing to take us on for the duration."

Was this a roundabout way of asking if he could fill in a little longer? Tide them over to the next minister? "What duration are we talking about? A month? Two?"

Bert gave him an odd look. "However long God leads you to stay on as our permanent pastor."

Garrett straightened in his chair. "You're asking me—?"

"We're muddling this all up, Garrett," Bert apologized. "Julian and I are here on behalf of the church board to offer you a permanent pastorship for as long as you want to be here or until God leads you elsewhere. Complete with a raise, health insurance and a retirement program."

Garrett blinked. They were offering him a job?

"That's what took us so long to make this offer," Julian added. "We didn't want to commit to benefits we couldn't deliver, but that's been taken care of now. Offerings are up since you came on board, and we've now worked out the paperwork and legalities involved."

"We wish we could offer you a parsonage, though." Bert gave him a regretful look. "You know, so you wouldn't have to keep boarding with the Lovells. We had to sell off our parsonage to make ends meet after the last economic downturn."

Garrett could only stare at them, trying in vain to process all that they were saying.

Julian chuckled. "You know, Bert, I think we've left Garrett speechless for the first time in his life."

Bert smiled, too. "So what do you say, Pastor McCrae? When you originally interviewed, you'd mentioned furthering your education. We can be flexible—maybe even assist financially as you pursue an advanced degree."

They wanted him to *stay*? Offering a raise? Assistance with his education?

"I am," he said slowly, "as Julian pointed out, entirely speechless."

Stunned, to be exact. This new direction was out of the blue. He hadn't considered it as an option. All along he thought Old Man Moppert and a few long-entrenched, hard-to-please others would ensure he'd be out of here by year's end.

Bert leaned forward. "Are you willing to take us on?"

"To be quite honest, I don't know what to say. This offer is, to say the least, unexpected."

Bert gave Julian an I-told-you-so look. "Our wives said we should discuss this with you early on, even if we didn't have all the details worked out. That you might be making other plans. You haven't, have you?"

"Actually, I have.

"That big-city church you interned at wants you back, right?"

"No, but I have another venture under consideration."

"So have we lost out? A day late and a dollar short?" Julian's shoulders slumped. "Oh, man, Marisela and Staci aren't going to be happy with us."

Suddenly uncomfortable, Garrett rose and moved to stand behind his chair, gripping the padded back. "I'm afraid I've long had my heart set on mission work, gentlemen."

Then why did this unexpected offer fill him with such an incredible joy, tug so insistently at his spirit? Had Drew been right? This was his calling? Or did the fact that he'd instantly thought of how staying in Hunter Ridge might enable a future with Jodi prove this was yet another test to be passed, to prove his mettle and strengthen his resolve? Mission work in remote areas of the world wasn't for the indecisive. God had to know He could count on you.

Julian perked up. "We can provide opportunities for you in hands-on missions work if that's what you're looking for. Like building homes in Mexico or doing projects on the Arizona reservations. We might even be able to foot the bill for a short-term overseas trip on down the road.

You know, with one of those ministries Drew's so involved in."

These guys were *serious*. They sincerely wanted to keep him here. But did God want him to turn them down flat? Close the door on temptation and settle it right now, once and for all?

Bert raised a brow. "If you haven't made a final decision on anything, would you at least agree to pray about it? Give God a chance to weigh in? Maybe give us a word of hope to take back to the board—and our wives?"

What would it sound like to these fine men if a minister bluntly said no, he wasn't willing to pray about it? They had him over a barrel. And he could hardly say he'd pray about it and then *not* pray about it, even if he thought he already had a good idea how God felt about this one.

He gripped the back of the chair more tightly. "I'd be willing to do that."

Both men stood, and Bert thrust out his hand for a shake. "No hurry. No pressure. Take all the time you need."

Still overwhelmed, Garrett also shook Julian's hand. "I thank you both for your support."

"Not just us, Pastor. The whole board. And, except for a few members who shall remain nameless—although a man with your spiritual discernment can probably guess the outliers—the membership will welcome you with open arms."

"I'm sincerely humbled."

"We're grateful you'll give our offer your prayerful consideration." Bert gave him a quick nod. "We'd love to keep you, Pastor McCrae, but we want you to be firm in God's will should you decide to accept."

When they departed, Garrett closed the door, then dropped into the chair behind his desk, overwhelmed. He'd had it in his head for so long that God called him to fill the role Drew had been forced to abandon. Despite denials to Drew, Jodi and Grandma Jo, he'd harbored a certainty that in some small way he could make up for the part he'd played in the tragedy that robbed his friend of a long-held dream.

Then Jodi had unexpectedly reappeared on his doorstep—the girl, now a woman, he'd never quite gotten over. He was more drawn to her these past two weeks than ever before. She knew him like no one else did—the good and the bad.

And he'd turned her away.

He'd pushed her away because of a commitment to what he'd been so sure he'd been called to. Was this job offer at Christ's Church a test from God? A temptation of the enemy to lure him away from God's best? Or an answer to the prayers of a lonely man who deeply desired to follow his Heavenly Father's leading?

He leaned back in the chair and closed his eyes.

He had a lot of hours of prayer and scripture meditation ahead of him.

He *had* to get this one right.

"Garrett's going to be amazed when he finds out what happened," a smiling Sofia said as she, Jodi and nine other ladies from the church finished loading—to the gills—six vehicles parked outside the church.

Garrett *would* be amazed, that is, if he joined them on their trek. He'd originally planned to come along this morning—but that was before he'd made a U-turn in their relationship. Jodi wasn't ready to face him.

"The mothers are going to be thrilled with all of this." Sunshine Carston waved her hand toward the SUV next to her, an early wedding gift from her husband-to-be. "And the volunteers at Canyon Springs Christian should be able to beat the Pacific storm front that's supposed to push in tonight."

"You've done a great job on this project, Jodi," Delaney Hunter called to her. "Even without last night's unexpected boon, it would still be a respectable Merry Christmas for gals who need to know they're loved."

"I can't accept all the credit." Jodi secured the canvas tarp covering the pickup bed's contents. "Like the saying goes, it takes a village."

"That it does," a male voice chimed in from where Garrett was helping a bundled-up Dolly out a side door of the church. The ladies cheered as their much-loved pastor put in an appearance.

In spite of herself, Jodi's heart gave a happy leap, which she immediately tamped down. Now that she was considering a move to Hunter Ridge, it was just as well that Garrett wouldn't be ministering at the church here. How could she bear to see him on a regular basis?

Perhaps today, though, she'd have an opportunity to apologize. To find a few minutes to again ask his forgiveness for betraying a confidence and to assure him it had never been her intention to draw him away from God's plan for his life. Not that another apology would change anything between them. He'd made his decision. But maybe it would ease the ache in her heart.

Marisela put her hands on her hips. "We thought you might be skipping out on us, Pastor."

"You know me better than that." Garrett wagged a playful finger at her, then surveyed the cars, SUVs and pickups. "So everything's loaded? You don't need my Explorer?"

Delaney shook her head at her cousin-in-law. "Nope, this does it, even with last night's surprise bonanza."

"A surprise?"

He focused a curious look on Jodi. Was he

wondering why she hadn't called to share the news with him? Quickly she filled him in on her phone call with Melody.

He chuckled at the end of the tale. "So it was at her house this whole time?"

She nodded, enjoying the dumbfounded look on Garrett's face.

He laughed. "Does God work in mysterious ways, or what?"

"He does."

"Amazing. So, then, ladies—" His merry gaze now embraced the others. "Since my SUV isn't needed, the least I can do is drive one of the vehicles." He held out his hand to Jodi. "Keys, please."

He was going to drive hers? Was she expected to ride along with him, or ride with one of the other volunteers?

"You go in the middle, Jodi." Dolly gave her a push toward Rio's truck. "I want to be where I can grip the armrest in case Garrett takes a curve too fast. That boy still doesn't understand what a brake pedal is for."

The others laughed and moved toward their respective vehicles, but Jodi hesitated—until Garrett jerked his head in the direction of the truck to indicate she was to go before him.

How awkward. But she'd be squeezing three into the front seat of any of the other vehicles, too, and it might draw unwanted attention if she refused to ride with Garrett and Dolly in her own truck.

When he'd opened the passenger-side door, she reluctantly climbed inside, then searched for her seat belt as he helped Dolly aboard.

"All in?" He slammed the side door and strode around the front of the truck to climb in. Then he squinted up at the lowering clouds. "Good thing we can get this done this morning."

Jodi nodded, uncomfortably conscious of Garrett's jacketed arm brushing hers as he buckled his seat belt. She could smell the leather of his jacket and the clean fresh scent of his aftershave—and scooted a tiny bit in Dolly's direction.

The older woman patted her arm. "I imagine you're enjoying your family."

"I am. It's been fun. My two brothers-in-law will be coming this afternoon instead of tomorrow, hoping to get in ahead of the snow. So the more the merrier. Although I wasn't originally sold on the idea, I'm glad that my sisters insisted we do this."

"Your grandmother certainly loved having you all here for the summers and holidays."

Jodi nodded, conscious of Garrett's listening ears. Grandma had loved it when he and his Grandma Jo visited, too. Except for that last time, of course, when she'd caught him teaching her granddaughter the fine art of kissing.

She shoved aside the memory. "It was a dream world that most kids don't get to enjoy now. So much more freedom. I'm thankful for the time I got to spend up here."

"As much as I once wanted to get away from this town," Garrett joined in as he took the caravan's lead out of the parking lot, "I can't imagine growing up anywhere else."

He might say that, but once again he could hardly wait to put the little community behind him. At least, though, he wasn't like so many who wandered aimlessly, who spent the majority of their lives trying to find a purpose.

The trip to Canyon Springs went quickly, with Garrett and Dolly doing most of the talking, only occasionally encouraging her to join in. Did Garrett find this as awkward as she did? Thankfully, not many knew that only a few days ago it appeared God might be drawing them together. How rapidly things had changed. If Dolly noticed anything out of kilter about their interactions today, she didn't let on.

Despite their falling-out, Garrett was still so, well, so *Garrett*. Bursting into song when the radio channel they'd been listening to piped up with an especially jazzy rendition of a Christmas carol, he elbowed her until he got her to join in. Even Dolly found herself nodding along with the beat. Just like old times, fun followed Garrett wherever he went.

Which left her feeling a little sad. Did he feel nothing, not even a twinge of downheartedness at having closed the door to her?

When they pulled into the parking lot at Canyon Springs Christian, Dolly gasped. "This looks just like a Christmas card, doesn't it?"

It did. The native stone building, set back in a stand of ponderosa pines, featured a cross atop its bell tower and a snow-covered roof that resembled that of an icing-topped gingerbread house.

With snow flurries now dancing in the air, Meg Diaz and other volunteers from the church joined those from Hunter Ridge in hauling in the gifts to be divvied up for distribution that afternoon.

Jodi caught up with Meg. "Where's Kara?"

Meg linked the fingers of both her hands and held them out in front of her like a rounded belly. "Her husband didn't want her out today for fear she'd slip and fall. For once Kara wasn't stubborn about it, so you can imagine how she's feeling right about now."

Not long ago, envy would have stabbed—and guilt would have gnawed. But today Jodi felt free. Clean. And filled with compassion for Kara's discomfort.

She glanced in Garrett's direction to find him watching her as he lifted a box from the back of the pickup. He dipped his head slightly and winked, almost as if he understood.

We would have made a good team, Lord.

But she wasn't going there today. No gloom fests. Today was about helping single moms, young women who were likely just as scared as she'd once been. Feeling just as stupid. Just as alone. Just as ashamed. Maybe even angry.

Among them would be young women like Kimmy who'd been kicked out when their family couldn't deal with the reality of their situation. At least Jodi knew with all her heart that her own family would never have kicked her out of their home.

Could she ever bring herself to tell them the truth of that difficult time in her life? Maybe. Someday. She'd certainly discuss it with her nieces if she suspected either was being pressured by a boy who claimed to love her. It might be, too, that she'd one day be called on to have a heart-to-heart with a teenage Henry.

As she carried another bag into the church, she couldn't help but glance in Garrett's direction as he hauled in one of the heavier items. On the drive over, he'd acted as if he didn't have a care in the world. But that wasn't true.

She still suspected that, like her, he needed to

be set free from the chains of guilt that bound him. But to do that, wouldn't he first need to admit that there were any chains at all?

Chapter Seventeen

No doubt about it, he was proud of Jodi.

With a Christmas tune playing quietly in the background on their return trip to Hunter Ridge, the gentle notes of a saxophone the perfect backdrop for the now steadily falling snow, he glanced over at Jodi who was chatting with Dolly about the best way to cook a turkey. He'd had Al drop it off at the Thorpe cabin yesterday, to her sisters' delight.

He wouldn't say anything to her about those proud feelings, of course. But she'd proven today how big the strides were that she'd made in the way she'd dealt with the unexpected arrival of a seventeen-year-old single mother with her infant and a very pregnant teenage mom-to-be. In fact, she'd gravitated to them, the peace now in her heart reflecting in her expression as she'd placed an arm around one of the girls. She'd even reached out to cradle the baby in her arms.

It would take time. There would undoubtedly be setbacks. More healing for God to do. But she was going to be okay. Someday God would send her a man worthy of her, a man who would be a father to *her* children. Drew? Man, as much as he loved his buddy, he sure hoped not.

Adjusting the windshield wiper speed, he refocused his thoughts, although not on anything any more comforting. He'd been up a good deal of the night, but still had no clear lead as to what he was to do. How could he be certain if leaving— or staying—was the right decision? His thoughts were muddled, that's for sure, but he knew God wasn't a God of confusion. He had to be patient, not rush in one direction or the other. Julian and Bert said to take his time. He needed to trust that God would find a way to clearly hammer home His preference.

"What's *your* preference, Garrett?"

Startled as the background conversation intruded on his thoughts, he turned to Dolly, her gaze fixed intently on him.

"Pardon?"

"What's your preference? Corn-bread dressing or cranberry-walnut stuffing?"

"Yes."

Jodi laughed, and his heart hummed at the sound. Dolly merely shook her head.

"Well, you asked, didn't you? I assumed you wanted an honest answer." He couldn't help but smile. He'd miss Dolly when—if—he left. She'd put up with a lot from him this past year. He'd forever treasure his time with her and her husband. Fifty years of marriage. Three kids. Seven grandkids. It was a joy to hang around couples who'd weathered the good times and the bad. People who knew how to put someone's best interests before their own, to love richer or poorer, in sickness and in health. Maybe some of their wisdom would rub off on him.

But could he honestly say, fully believe, that he'd ever be capable of meeting someone else's needs before his own? Or had he done that when he'd given Jodi back to God?

He glanced again at Jodi, who was gazing almost pensively out the side window. *Penny for your thoughts, pretty lady.*

Dolly had asked him, although unrelated to the thoughts drifting through his mind, what his preferences were. He couldn't deny he was beginning to have a few very distinct ones.

But he had to be sure.

"I thought Garrett would stop by today." The corners of Star's mouth turned downward as she dropped one-third of a cup of pancake batter into the hot nonstick pan. "The kids had so much fun building a snow fort with him the other day. I even felt like a kid again myself. And today—building snowmen, playing fox and geese and all the inside games. Those would have been even more fun if he'd have joined us, don't you think?"

Jodi smiled despite a melancholy tug at her heart as she glanced at the children crowded around the nativity scene, each holding a king or shepherd figurine as they journeyed them in their imaginations to Bethlehem. Just like she and Garrett used to do. "Life's always more fun when Garrett's around."

Star sighed as she lifted the edge of the pancake with a spatula and flipped it over. Nice and golden. "I don't see how he could resist the promise of pumpkin pancakes this evening—he has to eat sometime, doesn't he? And how could that obviously smitten man miss out on another opportunity to see *you*?"

She wasn't ready to tell the family that a romantic relationship that had sprung to life so quickly had already withered and died. Ironically, her visit to Hunter Ridge had originally been motivated by not wanting to put a damper on her family's holiday. Now this.

"Come on, Star. It's Christmas Eve. I imagine

today's been packed for him. I had no illusions that we'd see him beyond a glimpse in the pulpit tonight."

Jodi dipped into the batter bowl and poured a dollop into her own heated pan. Pumpkin pancakes before the Christmas Eve service was a tradition at the cabin, and it took teamwork to prepare enough for the hungry household. Then after the service, they'd return for a family time around the tree—reading the Christmas story, singing favorite songs, and sharing a bedtime snack of chocolate chip cookies and hot chocolate.

Oh, and each opening one present.

She'd already slipped one away that she'd earlier placed under the tree for Garrett. Maybe she'd mail the gloves once his plans were firm. Even desert regions could be bitterly cold.

"Tomorrow, then." Star gave a conclusive nod as she slid a pancake onto the almost-filled platter, then again dipped the measuring cup into the batter.

"Don't count on it."

Star frowned. "Why not?"

"You forget, sis, he has family here in town, and they have their own gatherings and traditions."

"Oh, pooh. Doesn't the Bible say a man shall leave his mother—"

Star had already assumed that there was something of a more lasting nature between her and Garrett. She'd obviously seen *something* there. At least Jodi could take consolation that she hadn't imagined it—although that was a pretty sorry solace.

"Mmm. This smells incredible." Star's husband Mac joined them to lean in and snatch a piece of crisp bacon off the warming tray, then kissed his wife's cheek.

Star all but purred at the attention. "We're almost ready to eat. Where are Ronda and Jon?"

Mac lowered his voice. "I think they're trying to get the you-know-what assembled."

"Well, tell them to get on in here and take care of that later. Jodi already has the table set. Doesn't it look great? Just like Grandma used to do."

He stepped back to inspect the festive arrangements. The sun had already dipped behind the silhouetted ponderosas, the fat candles in the lanterns lending a homey glow to the mismatched china, cloth napkins, and red-and-green plaid tablecloth. "Sure wish I could have experienced a bit of your childhood. My grandma thought holidays were an excuse to eat out or cater in."

Jodi cringed. If not for Garrett, that's exactly what they'd be doing.

Star cast her an impish look, then slid her final pancake onto the waiting stack, and Jodi did the same. She wasn't looking forward to tonight's Christmas Eve service, but there was no way to get out of it without drawing her family's unwanted attention to the disappointing outcome of a relationship that had such a short time ago seemed so promising.

Happy holidays, everyone.

How could she bear seeing Garrett up front tonight, all the while knowing that he didn't have room in his big heart for her?

What a day.

His cell phone pressed to his ear, Garrett gathered his Bible from the dresser top as he prepared to head off to the church. He was running late. Again.

"You're more than welcome, Dick. Gotta keep those kids of yours toasty warm. And Merry Christmas to you, too."

He pocketed his cell phone with a smile. While he'd have preferred the utility company hadn't mentioned his name, making arrangements for overdue bill payment for a couple who had fallen on hard times was an expense he was more than happy to cover.

He'd just opened the door to the coat closet in the living room when his cell phone rang again. He placed his Bible on a nearby chair and jerked his jacket off a hanger, still managing to answer on the third ring.

"Mr. McCrae?" a youthful male voice asked tentatively.

"You got him."

"Me and my friends—we got home before dark. Our folks thought we should let you know. Thanks for stopping to help us."

On his way back from Canyon Springs, having dropped off an elderly church member who feared driving on bad roads but wanted to spend Christmas with his sister and her family, he'd spotted a carload of teenagers at the side of the road. Out of gas.

"You're welcome. Jake, was it? I'm glad to hear you made it safe and sound."

"We hope you have a Merry Christmas."

"I'm counting on it. Merry Christmas to all of you, too."

He again shoved his phone into his pocket, then glanced at his watch and groaned. It was a little hard to sneak in late when you sat at the front of the church. He'd spent much of the day, though, putting out fires, so to speak. Usually with the arrival of Christmas Eve day, the hectic aspects of the holidays settled down. But not this year.

Nor had today been spent as he'd originally envisioned only a few days ago. He couldn't count the times his thoughts turned to Jodi and her family. Wondering what they were doing, if the kids had missed him as they made another snowman—and how those pumpkin pancakes they always had on Christmas Eve would have tasted.

But he had only himself to blame for being left out.

He'd taken his eyes off the ball, so to speak, allowed himself to get sidetracked when Jodi arrived in town. He should have thought it through better before getting carried away and suggesting they give God a chance to see where He wanted them to go. *He'd* already been told, hadn't he? Nevertheless, he'd let himself play with fire. Got his hopes up—and probably Jodi's—about finding a way for him to manipulate God's plans.

He slipped his arms into his jacket sleeves and adjusted the collar. Now another unexpected twist threatened to derail him. He'd promised Bert and Julian he'd take the offer under prayerful consideration. But nothing had changed since yesterday, had it? Not really. He was still a man with a purpose—one that didn't include Jodi or a local pastorship. God hadn't changed His mind, and neither should he.

So why didn't he feel at peace with that?

And had he, truly, ever felt a peace about it? He'd long told himself the restlessness, the underlying disquiet, would go away. That peace would come after he got through Bible college. Got through this interim pastorship.

It would come once he was released from here and on the mission field, right? That confirmation?

Leaning into the closet, he pulled his guitar case from the back. He hadn't played in a while and should probably have carved out some time to practice today. Too late now, though.

"Don't you look handsome." In her coat, boots and gloves, Dolly paused in the living room doorway to gaze at him with a smile. While he wasn't in a suit, he'd topped the forest-green cashmere sweater his folks had given him as an early Christmas present with a tan corduroy sports jacket. And a tie. "You should dress up more often. I imagine Jodi would agree wholeheartedly."

Was Dolly feeling him out? Sensing that something had subtly changed since only a handful of nights ago when she and Al had helped him and Jodi decorate the cabin? But he didn't want to talk about Jodi.

"Thanks for the vote of approval." He zipped the jacket up to his neck, then pulled his gloves from his pockets. "Are you sure you and Al don't want a ride? It's getting kind of nasty out there."

"He's warming up the car, and we'll be right behind you."

With a quick kiss to her cheek, he headed out the door, Bible and guitar in hand. When he arrived at the church, he paused before exiting his vehicle to take in the Kinkade-like scene. Stained glass windows glowed through the steadily falling snow, and a troupe of faithful worker bees, shovels in hand, were busy keeping the sidewalks and steps cleared for those arriving.

Unless the Heavenly referee blew His whistle before Garrett turned down the church's offer at the conclusion of tonight's service, this would be his last Christmas in Hunter Ridge for who knew how long. Maybe forever. When he'd returned to town a year ago, not particularly happy about it but determined to yield to God's—and Grandma Jo's—will, he hadn't expected to feel a tug at his heart as he prepared to leave.

Assuming she came to this service and tomorrow's as well, tonight would be one of his final glimpses of Jodi, too. But he wasn't surprised at the heart tug accompanying that realization.

"There you are." Marisela called with a smile as he stepped inside the main door. She and her husband, whom she nudged with her elbow, were greeters tonight. "Bert here was afraid he might have to get out his harmonica, so we're both glad to see you here—and with that guitar of yours."

"Can you play 'Silent Night' on that harmonica, Bert?"

The older man's smile widened. "You betcha."

"Plan on it, then. We'll close with a duet."

Bert's eyebrows rose, but Garrett patted him on the back and headed into the dimly lit church. Good folks, the Palmers.

Once settled on the platform, though, his heart momentarily stalled when he spied Jodi—beautiful in the soft candlelight—sitting near the front next to Drew, with her family members filling the pew on her other side.

You're not making this easy on me, Lord.

As Sofia's gifted fingers on the piano keys filled the hallowed space with the sweet notes of "O Come, O Come Emmanuel," he momentarily closed his eyes. Drawing in the faint scent of pine from the beribboned swags of evergreen branches, he endeavored to focus his thoughts on this holy time of year. On the gift of God's son.

Julian Gonzales, not only a church board member but a talented vocalist, followed Garrett's opening prayer with a moving solo of "What Child Is This?"—then led the congregation in song after worshipful song. A cluster of giggling grade school children followed, crowding onto the platform to recite "pieces" he'd memorized himself when their age, and then it was his turn to speak.

In spite of good intentions, he hadn't much

time to prepare the message. The past several days had been filled with activity. With prayer.

As he gripped the edges of the lectern, he gazed out over the congregation. His Grandma Jo was over there with his sister's two kids on one side and cousin Luke's little Chloe on the other. And seated next to the little girl, Luke's Travis and his girlfriend. Travis's oldest sister, Anna, too, who, like Jodi, was shedding her tomboyish ways.

Newlyweds Luke and Delaney smiled back at him, and Grady had his arm comfortably around his fiancée's shoulders, Sunshine's kindergarten-aged daughter Tessa snuggled in at his other side. Then close by, Sunshine's best friend, Tori Janner, who was almost a part of the little family that would unite in an upcoming Valentine's Day wedding.

Uncle Dave and a somewhat frail-looking Aunt Elaine, a sparkling turban on her head, looked into each other's eyes, savoring each day together that God granted them. His gaze slowly passed over other uncles and aunts. Cousins. His own folks. A sanctuary full of people, many of whom he'd known since childhood. People he'd come to love this past year.

He'd miss them all.

Even Randall Moppert.

With a smile tugging, he cleared his throat and bowed his head. "Please join me in prayer."

He couldn't have told anyone afterward exactly what he'd said to God during that prayer—or in the message that followed. But he spoke from the depths of his heart during both, filled with a deep thankfulness. His message was of God's love for His creation, a message of the redeeming miracle of Jesus's birth and ultimate sacrifice on the cross, a message of the hope yet to come at His promised return.

God willing, his words would continue to impact hearts here long after he'd moved on from this pastorship.

At the conclusion of his message, he reached for his guitar and motioned to Bert to join him on the platform. As the delicate opening notes of "Silent Night" whispered to the farthest corner of the hushed sanctuary, he again looked out on the people of this church. Christ's Church.

"Silent night, holy night…"

Now standing, the congregation joined him, softly at first, then with an increasing power that echoed through the candlelit space.

"All is calm, all is bright…"

He drew in a breath, his heart weighing heavy with an unknown future stretching before him.

"Round yon virgin, mother and child. Holy infant so tender and mild…"

He swallowed as his eyes drank in the faces of those before him. His folks. Drew. The beautiful Jodi…

The people of Christ's Church.

His church. *His* community.

In that moment, as he quietly picked the strings of his guitar, a tingling sensation curled up the nape of his neck. And peace—that precious, promised peace that passes all understanding— finally pushed its way in to settle into his heart, the beacon he'd long awaited to guide him.

Tears pricked his eyes, but he blinked them away. God had spoken, and this time he was listening.

"Sleep in heavenly peace…"

Chapter Eighteen

It was getting late.

It was already ten thirty, the cabin having finally settled down for the night with giggling kids tucked in their sleeping bags on cots in the attic room above and the couples having slipped off to their own rooms.

She'd be on the sofa again, not bothering to pull out its folding mattress and make up the bed. At least that morning at the grocery store she'd finally found a baby Jesus to substitute for the one she hadn't yet found. Granted, it was a cheap plastic version and only half the size it should have been, but maybe it wouldn't matter to the kids?

As silence descended on the cabin that held so many happy memories—new ones made tonight—she finished cleaning up in the kitchen. Her nieces and nephew had loved the grab-bag gifts. Silly, inexpensive little items, but you'd have thought she'd spent a fortune based on the delight they'd been greeted with. And not a single electronic item among them!

They'd shared warm cookies and cocoa before gathering once again around the brightly lit Christmas tree, taking turns to select a song that would be sung next. The evening wrapped up with Mac reading the Christmas story to sleepy-eyed children—and bedtime hugs and kisses.

Although she'd felt God close throughout this family-filled day, when the couples, hand in hand, had gone off to their own rooms, she struggled to hold back the sense of aloneness that assailed her.

Grabbing a dampened dishcloth, she vigorously wiped down the countertop. *I will not have a pity party tonight.*

But how could she stop thinking of Garrett? Her heart had ached when he'd stepped to the lectern this evening, looking sharp in a green sweater and sports jacket—and tie. She'd had to smother a smile at the memory of a ponytailed teenager who'd cruised around town on a motorcycle that her grandma had forbidden her to ride.

What Grandma didn't know, though, hadn't hurt her…right?

Again an unbidden smile tugged as she put away the silverware and wiped down the dish drainer. At least if she landed that job Brooke had told her about, she could live right here in this much-loved cabin. And with Garrett no longer the local pastor, she could fit comfortably into her new church home, too.

But I'd thought for sure, Lord...

At the sound of soft tapping, she paused to listen. Had one of the kids decided to sneak back downstairs? Then the sound came again—more persistent—and this time she pinpointed it. The back door of the mudroom.

Drying off her hands, she slipped into the adjoining room and drew back the curtain to peep out.

Garrett?

Her heart gave a happy leap, but she quickly tamped down rising hope. He probably wanted to make things right between them. To tie up any loose ends of misunderstanding before he left town. Saying a silent prayer for wisdom, she opened the door.

"Hey, Jodi."

He sounded so casual, his words no different from the many times she'd opened this door to him throughout their growing-up years.

"Hey, Garrett."

"I know it's late." His words came softly, no doubt noting the darkened cabin when he'd approached. "But I was hoping you'd still be up."

"I'm winding down." Her own words were

whispered. "Just straightening things in the kitchen so all will be ready for tomorrow."

"I'm sorry I couldn't get here earlier." He glanced off into the snowy night, then back at her. "If this isn't a good time, I can—"

"No, no, this is fine." She stepped back to motion him inside. She may as well get this over with. Perhaps offer the apology that she'd never had the opportunity to make—to assure him she'd never intended to challenge his calling, to stand in the way of God's leading. "Everyone's tucked in for the night."

"That must have been quite a feat settling down the troops." He shut the door behind him. "Especially Henry. That kid has energy to burn."

Just like his "Uncle" Garrett?

"I think we wore them out today, then let them stay up a bit later than usual. My sisters are so set on making lasting memories for them of the cabin. But no matter how much we try, it's not quite the same without Grandma and Grandpa."

"No, it wouldn't be. But there are times, you know, to cherish the past, yet make way for the future."

Was he alluding to *their* past? That they needed to treasure it for what it was—the good times of their childhood—and not mourn what could never be?

"I thought you might like to know," he continued, "that right after tonight's service, Trey Kenton texted that Kara had their little girl."

"Ahh. A Christmas Eve baby."

"And speaking of babies..." He pulled off his gloves and placed them on the countertop, then reached into his pocket to pull out a little gift bag. "I bought you something and wanted to make sure you got it tonight."

He emptied the bag into the palm of his hand.

A tiny plastic Jesus.

"Garrett, thank you. I still haven't found Grandma's." She took the infant from his hand, identical to the one she'd found and tucked away for morning. But she wouldn't tell him that. His thoughtfulness touched her too deeply to spoil his gift.

"I looked all over for something more substantial." He gazed down at the holy child almost self-consciously. "You know, sized to match your grandma's, but..."

"No, this is perfect. The crib won't be empty. Thank you." But her heart ached as she cradled the child in her hand.

He glanced at the open door from which the Christmas tree lights illuminated the small mudroom. Then he gave it a push to slightly close it, apparently not intending for the whole house to hear what he had to say.

"I also came to apologize, Jodi."

She shook her head. She hadn't expected that. "No, Garrett, I owe *you* an apology."

His brow crinkled. "How do you figure?"

"Because it was never my intention to hold you back from where God has told you He wants you to go. That wasn't Drew's intention, either. He didn't want you driven by guilt, and I only saw what an amazing impact you're having on this church and community. But neither of us spent years in prayer, listening to God about it as you have. We had no right to an opinion. No right to challenge you."

"I…disagree."

"No, you were right. We were wrong."

"What I mean, Jodi, is as longtime friends you and Drew had every right under the sun to challenge me. To keep me from moving blindly forward. Not that God couldn't have used me on a foreign mission field. I know He would have. He could take it and bless it even if I'd gone for all the wrong reasons."

A tingle of disquiet rippled through her. "You're talking past tense, Garrett."

And thoroughly confusing her.

"Tonight God showed me that in my blind determination to go to the Middle East, I'd been running away from His good and perfect will. Not toward it."

"I don't understand."

The corners of his mouth lifted as he looked intently into her eyes. "I've been offered a full-time ministry position at Christ's Church, Jode. And I've accepted it."

Her breath caught. "Are you certain, Garrett? You're not just letting Drew's and my all-too-human doubts influence you?"

He shook his head. "At first, I thought you both were flat-out wrong. That God was testing me to see if I'd turn aside at the first opposition. I was determined not to let that happen. I took offense at what I perceived as your and Drew's interference. So I apologize. I'm sorry if I hurt you."

"Don't apologize. We may have grown up as best friends, but too many years have passed to give me the right to insert myself into your decision-making after having only recently become reacquainted."

"But in many ways, it's been an amazing reacquaintance, hasn't it?" He tilted his head in question.

"It has." Or at least it had until their falling out.

"So to answer your question, yes, I'm certain about committing to the church. To Hunter Ridge. Everywhere I turned the past two days God's confronted me with people not only in need, but people who need *me*. As hard as I tried at first to shut out the implications of that, tonight it was as if God opened my eyes to see what you and Drew had seen. That my life, as impossible as it seems, is making a difference right here in my old hometown."

"He's confirmed the direction you're to take?"

"Rock solid." He placed his hand over his heart. "He's given me that elusive piece to the puzzle that I'd longed for. The piece I thought would fall into place once I escaped this town, once I got away from the reminder of Drew's accident and off on a mission field. I thought that then, somehow, some way, I'd be absolved for the part I played in his injuries."

"Drew said it wasn't your fault."

"Maybe not my fault in that it wasn't a premeditated attempt to injure him. But I should have been more cautious."

"Drew said you *both* got carried away, were goofing off."

"And which of us, do you think, has the longest track record of that?"

"He accepts the responsibility. You didn't make him jump into the water."

"No, but—"

"Let it go, Garrett. I know from my own experience that the hardest thing in the world is to forgive ourselves even when God and others already have. Didn't I hear a very recent Sunday message on this very topic? And someone wise once told me that being unwilling to forgive myself was akin to taking Jesus's sacrificial gift and tossing it in the trash."

Garrett flinched. "Someone wise told you that, did he?"

"Yep."

"You think I should take his advice?"

"I would."

He paused to think a moment—pray?—and she could hear the cabin walls creak. A window rattle. The wind had picked up.

"So you have peace about staying, Garrett?" She had to be sure. Sure that she hadn't aborted God's plan for his life.

"An amazing peace. It hit me during the Christmas Eve service tonight as I looked out across the sea of faces. My family. Yours. Drew. Members and visitors. My heart swelled with a love so powerful, a peace and sense of purpose so overwhelming, I can't even describe it to you. I know that feelings ebb and flow, but I'll always remember this night. Will commemorate it in my heart. I've prayed for this peace, this confirmation of my calling for five years…and now tonight God sent it. Until He tells me differently, this is where I want to invest my life."

A ripple of joy coursed through her. And yet…

"I'm happy for you, Garrett. You will make—are already making—a difference in this town."

"It won't be easy, though."

"God doesn't always call us to do easy, does He?"

"Seldom. But God also revealed to me tonight one thing that would make it a significantly less painful journey." He gently took the baby Jesus from her and placed it next to his gloves. Then as he looked deeply into her eyes, he took her hand in his. "Marry me, Jodi. Marry the new pastor of Christ's Church of Hunter Ridge."

Her eyes widened as all the doubts she'd soothed herself with the past few days—reasons she'd never make a good minister's wife and how God knew that all along—assailed her.

"I...I can't play the piano."

He laughed, his hand tightening on hers. "Or cook? Keep house? Or teach little kids in Sunday school?"

"None of those things. Not very well, anyway."

"To be perfectly honest, Jodi, I'm a pretty good cook, if I do say so myself. Enjoy it actually—if you'd do the cleanup. Sofia's got the piano playing covered. Marisela's backup. And all the Sunday school slots are currently filled. So even if you'd want to, you'd have to wait awhile to get your foot in the door."

"But—"

"Jodi, I love you. I think I've loved you ever since we were kids. Loved you even when you literally gave me a kick in the seat of the pants that sent me sprawling into the dust. I just...I can't imagine life without you in it."

Words she'd only dreamed of hearing.

"I've loved you for as long as I can remember, Garrett. I never dreamed until earlier this week that you might feel the same about me."

"Then it looks like, Jodi, you owe me an answer to my question."

"You posed a question? It was worded more like an order."

"I'm a desperate man, besotted with the woman I love—and scared to death she'll walk away and never look back." He tugged her closer. "So *will* you marry me? We could buy this cabin from your folks and settle in for a happily-ever-after. I even promise to be on my best behavior, too."

She clucked her tongue. "I'm not so sure about that."

"I will. I promise."

"What I mean is, I like you just the way you are." She looked disapprovingly at the uncharacteristic presence of his tie. "I don't want to wake up some morning next to a stranger."

"So is that a yes? Or do I need to get down on my knees and beg?" He dropped to one knee, again clasping her hand. "Will you marry me, Jodi?"

"I will."

Slowly he rose to his feet, his eyes not leaving hers. It didn't take coaxing on his part for Jodi to step into his open arms. But Garrett's lips had barely touched hers when something behind her crashed to the floor with a startling clatter. She spun to see an old tin that Grandma kept on the mudroom shelf, its lid popped off to expose cotton batting stuffed inside.

She pulled away from Garrett and knelt to pull out a cotton-wrapped object. The moment she held it in her hands, her suspicions were confirmed. "You're not going to believe this, Garrett."

She carefully unfolded the cotton. Then, cradling its precious contents in the palm of her hand, she stood and turned to her husband-to-be. "Baby Jesus."

Garrett reverently touched the tiny wooden figurine. The one they'd searched so long and hard for. His eyes then narrowed as he glanced suspiciously at the open shelf behind her. "How did that tin work its way to the edge of the shelf to fall off *right now*?"

She gazed in wonder at the baby in her hand. "It's tempting to think Grandma's given us a seal of approval, isn't it?"

"I'd be more inclined to suspect," Garrett said, shaking his head with a smile, "that she requested a diversion before things got too hot to handle in here."

"You think?"

He gently took baby Jesus and laid Him and the cotton batting next to the plastic one. Then he reached for her hand and tugged her close to gaze into her eyes. Gave a sigh of resignation.

"I love you, Jodi. And as much as I'd like to see how fast we could steam up those windows, out of respect for your grandma, I'd better get going."

"But you just got here." She wasn't ready to let him go. Not yet. Not ever.

His eyes twinkled as he released her hand and reached for his gloves. "It's late—and there's plenty of time in our future for steamy."

She laughed. He was right.

A lifetime.

Her heart dancing in anticipation, Jodi kissed him on the cheek. "But let it be known that I cast my vote for a *short* engagement."

Epilogue

Jodi nestled into the warmth of her sleeping bag, staring into the darkness from her nest on one of the living room couches.

Wide-awake on Christmas morning.

She was worse than a kid—all eyes and ears long before the sun would get around to crawling up over the horizon.

Garrett said he'd see her today. *But when?*

It had been all she could do last night not to bang on closed doors and announce to all what had taken place between her and Garrett. But before he'd stepped into the snowy night, he'd said he wanted to be there when she shared the news. Thankfully, everyone had already gone to bed or she couldn't have managed it. Her glowing face would have been a dead giveaway.

Smiling, she snuggled down deeper in her warm cocoon, relishing the pungent scent of the shadowed Christmas tree, the hint of wood smoke from the banked fire.

After Garrett had departed last night, she'd slipped baby Jesus into his manger. There she'd knelt for quite some time, the radiance from the Christmas tree lights reflecting the praise and wonder that overflowed from her heart. With reluctance, she'd finally unplugged the lights and crept into her makeshift bed. But she'd lain awake for who knows how long, savoring Garrett's words and treasuring the moments he'd held her in his arms.

He wants to marry me.

His tomboy childhood pal. A buddy who'd punched him and kicked him, competed with him, and shared more adventures than she could count. A friend who'd loved him to pieces with her little-kid heart. A woman who'd later made so many mistakes and harbored doubts as to God's love for much too long.

A sound from outside caught Jodi's ears and she tensed, straining to hear. Gravel on the driveway?

Instantly, she was on her feet, wrapping the sleeping bag around her sweatsuit-clad shoulders and thankful for the cozy socks the kids had given her last night. Heading to the front window, she peeped into the wintry night where a softly illuminating snow glow reflected off the lowered clouds.

Her heart leaped at the sight of Garrett's SUV, headlights off, creeping as silently as possible up the drive.

He'd come, just as promised.

She spun away from the window, then abruptly halted. Reindeer-faced socks and a velour sweatsuit. No makeup. Hair mussed from a restless, almost sleepless night. What a scary sight to greet her future husband.

Husband. She liked the sound of that.

Heart racing, she tossed the sleeping bag on the sofa and quietly hurried to the bathroom to finger-comb her hair and swish around a capful of mouthwash. Pinched her cheeks to add a bit of color. She reached the mudroom door and opened it just as Garrett stepped up on the porch.

"You came." Her words weren't but a breathless whisper as the frosty air swirled in around her ankles.

He slipped silently inside and closed the door behind him, then in the dim light drew her close to touch his warm lips to hers.

She nearly melted on the spot. *Last night hadn't been a dream.*

When he finally pulled back slightly, she could hear the smile in his voice. "Merry Christmas, Jodi Thorpe."

"Merry Christmas, Garrett McCrae."

"I didn't sleep a wink. How about you?"

"Well, maybe one. Or two."

He chuckled. "We're quite a pair, aren't we? I apologize for getting here so early, but I—"

She placed a silencing finger momentarily to his mouth. Then gave him a playful kiss. "I thought you'd never get here."

His hands tightened on her waist, his tone suddenly serious. "You know, I got to thinking after I left here. I sort of sprang all this on you last night. Out of the blue. I didn't even bring a ring. Or consider your career plans. If you need more time to think about it…"

Jodi tensed. Surely after the breathtaking greeting he'd just given her, he wasn't having second thoughts, was he? Getting cold feet? She grasped the lapels of his jacket and tugged lightly. "I'm already taking steps to obtain a work-from-home job, so if you're thinking of weaseling out of this, it's too late, Pastor."

She felt the rumble of silent laughter under her hands.

"No weaseling going on here. I wanted to make sure you're good with this. I can be pushy sometimes. I've always liked to get my own way."

"No foolin'." He wasn't telling her anything she didn't already know.

He was silent for a long moment, and overhead she could hear the creak of the attic floor. He tilted his head to listen as well.

"Sounds as if the troops may be stirring." He took one of her hands in his. "Are you ready to announce our engagement to your family?"

With her free hand, she poked him in the chest. "Just try to stop me."

"No way. I seem to recall a time when that got me wrestled to the ground and my mouth filled with dirt."

Jodi winced. What a brat she'd been. "I did do that, didn't I? I'm sorry."

"Now don't you start apologizing or we'll be standing here all day while I confess my own youthful sins."

The glow of Christmas tree lights suddenly illuminated the mudroom as the strains of "Joy to the World" from Grandma's old Mitch Miller Christmas sing-along CD filled the air.

"My sisters are up." Tears unexpectedly pricked her eyes. "That music was always the signal for us that it was okay to come down the stairs and open presents."

Garrett gently brushed away a tear trickling down her cheek. "You miss your grandma. I do, too."

She took a steadying breath and looked toward the adjoining room, the sound of childish laughter and the pounding of feet on the stairs echoing through the cabin. "I wish she could still be here to enjoy her great-grandchildren."

"Your sisters' kids, you mean?" His words came softly as he cupped her face in his hands. "Or *ours*?"

Startled, she gazed into his love-filled eyes. "Oh, *yes*, ours, too."

He nodded, satisfied, and then once again captured her mouth with his.

She giggled.

Blame it on the mudroom. Clearly, there would be a slight delay in making that engagement announcement.

* * * * *

If you loved this story, pick up the other
HEARTS OF HUNTER RIDGE *books,*
REKINDLING THE WIDOWER'S HEART
CLAIMING THE SINGLE MOM'S HEART
and these other stories of love
from fan-favorite author
Glynna Kaye
A CANYON SPRINGS COURTSHIP
PINE COUNTRY COWBOY
HIGH COUNTRY HOLIDAY

Available now from Love Inspired!

Find more great reads at
www.LoveInspired.com

Dear Reader,

Christmas. Such a special time of year as we're reminded of our Heavenly Father's precious gift of His son. Jesus, who fulfilled Biblical prophecy after prophecy to be the bridge between a loving God and His rebellious, straying children. Pause to think on that...the creator of the universe knows you by name and waits with open arms for you to turn to Him.

This season of joy and a budding romance, however, are dampened for childhood friends Jodi and Garrett as they struggle with doubts, emotional wounds and the bond of a guilty conscience. They know in their head that God provides a means of inner healing, forgiveness and restoration, but they must learn to accept those gifts into their heart to experience God's best for them.

Are you, too, bearing a burden of regret that weighs heavily at this holy season? Give it to God once and for all. You can trust that He's answered your prayer, for if we confess our sins, He is faithful and just and will forgive us our sins and purify us from all unrighteousness (1 John 1:9).

It's been such a joy to write a story set at Christmas while actually celebrating the Christmas season! Snowfall, Christmas music, family traditions and remembering the true reason for the season. Thank you for joining me in Jodi and Garrett's holiday journey to love. I pray you will have a very special Christmas, filled with that promised peace that passes all understanding.

You can contact me via email at glynna@glynnakaye.com or Love Inspired Books, 195 Broadway, 24th Floor, New York, NY 10007. Please visit my website at glynnakaye.com—and stop by loveinspiredauthors.com, seekerville.net, and seekerville.blogspot.com!

Glynna Kaye

LARGER-PRINT BOOKS!

GET 2 FREE
LARGER-PRINT NOVELS
PLUS 2 FREE
MYSTERY GIFTS

Love Inspired

SUSPENSE
RIVETING INSPIRATIONAL ROMANCE

Larger-print novels are now available...

REQUEST YOUR FREE BOOKS!
2 FREE WHOLESOME ROMANCE NOVELS IN LARGER PRINT
PLUS 2
FREE
MYSTERY GIFTS

※※※※※※※※※※※※※※※※※※※※

HEARTWARMING™

※※※※※※※※※※※※※※※※※※※※※※

Wholesome, tender romances

YES! Please send me 2 FREE Harlequin® Heartwarming Larger-Print novels and my 2 FREE mystery gifts (gifts worth about $10). After receiving them, if I don't wish to receive any more books, I can return the shipping statement marked "cancel." If I don't cancel, I will receive 4 brand-new larger-print novels every month and be billed just $5.24 per book in the U.S. or $5.99 per book in Canada. That's a savings of at least 19% off the cover price. It's quite a bargain! Shipping and handling is just 50¢ per book in the U.S. and 75¢ per book in Canada.* I understand that accepting the 2 free books and gifts places me under no obligation to buy anything. I can always return a shipment and cancel at any time. Even if I never buy another book, the two free books and gifts are mine to keep forever.

161/361 IDN GHX2

Name _____ (PLEASE PRINT) _____

Address _____ Apt. # _____

City _____ State/Prov. _____ Zip/Postal Code _____

Signature (if under 18, a parent or guardian must sign)

Mail to the **Reader Service:**
IN U.S.A.: P.O. Box 1867, Buffalo, NY 14240-1867
IN CANADA: P.O. Box 609, Fort Erie, Ontario L2A 5X3

* Terms and prices subject to change without notice. Prices do not include applicable taxes. Sales tax applicable in N.Y. Canadian residents will be charged applicable taxes. Offer not valid in Quebec. This offer is limited to one order per household. Not valid for current subscribers to Harlequin Heartwarming larger-print books. All orders subject to credit approval. Credit or debit balances in a customer's account(s) may be offset by any other outstanding balance owed by or to the customer. Please allow 4 to 6 weeks for delivery. Offer available while quantities last.

Your Privacy—The Reader Service is committed to protecting your privacy. Our Privacy Policy is available online at www.ReaderService.com or upon request from the Reader Service.

We make a portion of our mailing list available to reputable third parties that offer products we believe may interest you. If you prefer that we not exchange your name with third parties, or if you wish to clarify or modify your communication preferences, please visit us at www.ReaderService.com/consumerchoice or write to us at Reader Service Preference Service, P.O. Box 9062, Buffalo, NY 14240-9062. Include your complete name and address.

WESTERN WP PROMISES

YES! Please send me **The Western Promises Collection** in Larger Print. This collection begins with 3 FREE books and 2 FREE gifts (gifts valued at approx. $14.00 retail) in the first shipment, along with the other first 4 books from the collection! If I do not cancel, I will receive 8 monthly shipments until I have the entire 51-book Western Promises collection. I will receive 2 or 3 FREE books in each shipment and I will pay just $4.99 US/ $5.89 CDN for each of the other four books in each shipment, plus $2.99 for shipping and handling per shipment. *If I decide to keep the entire collection, I'll have paid for only 32 books, because 19 books are FREE! I understand that accepting the 3 free books and gifts places me under no obligation to buy anything. I can always return a shipment and cancel at any time. My free books and gifts are mine to keep no matter what I decide.

272 HCN 3070 472 HCN 3070

Name	(PLEASE PRINT)

Address	Apt. #

City	State/Prov.	Zip/Postal Code

Signature (if under 18, a parent or guardian must sign)

Mail to the **Reader Service:**

IN U.S.A.: P.O. Box 1867, Buffalo, NY 14240-1867
IN CANADA: P.O. Box 609, Fort Erie, Ontario L2A 5X3

* Terms and prices subject to change without notice. Prices do not include applicable taxes. Sales tax applicable in N.Y. Canadian residents will be charged applicable taxes. This offer is limited to one order per household. All orders subject to approval. Credit or debit balances in a customer's account(s) may be offset by any other outstanding balance owed by or to the customer. Please allow 4 to 6 weeks for delivery. Offer available while quantities last. Offer not available to Quebec residents.

READERSERVICE.COM

Manage your account online!

- Review your order history
- Manage your payments
- Update your address

We've designed the
Reader Service website
just for you.

Enjoy all the features!

- Discover new series available to you, and read excerpts from any series.
- Respond to mailings and special monthly offers.
- Connect with favorite authors at the blog.
- Browse the Bonus Bucks catalog and online-only exculsives.
- Share your feedback.

Visit us at:
ReaderService.com